Snowflakes & FIRE ESCAPES

J.M. Darhower

ISBN-10: 1942206100
ISBN-13: 978-1-942206-10-1

Previously published in the *All I Want* Anthology

Snowflakes & Fire Escapes
Cody Moran and Gracie Callaghan wanted nothing more than to escape the life they'd been born into, but it's the kind of life that doesn't like to let go. A story of love and heartache spanning the streets of Hell's Kitchen to far, far away, where it doesn't snow.

This isn't my life.

This freckle-faced, natural redhead with the ghastly pale skin that is splotched with red from the persistent sun... she isn't me. I'm not that girl who doesn't wear makeup, that girl who can't remember the last time her hair wasn't sloppily pulled up into a bun on the top of her head. I don't wear cut off jean shorts and flimsy tank tops and cheap two-dollar flip flops, my feet dirty and toe nails unpainted because there's just no reason to paint them anymore.

This isn't me.

It can't be.

It can't be.

Thick, dark sunglasses cover my once lively green eyes, partially because the sun is so goddamn blinding but mostly because I just don't want anyone to look at me anymore. I stand along the side of the northbound lane of Highway 77, beside my formerly reliable late model Chevy Malibu, watching as smoke rolls out from under the hood, and think about just how much this can't be happening.

I think about just how much this life isn't mine.

Just how much this person isn't me.

Sighing, I walk around to the passenger side of the car and yank the door open, the metal hinges groaning as I do. My fist bangs against the jammed glove box in the dash, the force making it pop right open. Fishing around inside, I pull out the heavy Motorola cell phone and flip it open, pushing the button to turn the ancient thing on.

There's only one person programmed into the

contacts. I press the button, dialing the number, and lean back against the side of the broken down car as it rings.

And rings.

And rings.

I'm about to hang up, to give up on finding any sort of help today, when the line clicks, the ringing stopping. "Hello."

"Hey, it's... uh..." I hesitate. "It's me... Grace."

The voice coming from these lips is timid. I don't like the way it sounds.

"Grace," he echoes, his tone steady and confident like mine used to be.

He doesn't ask me what I need.

He knows I'll get to it.

Eventually.

"Look, this car crapped out on me and I'm stuck out here on the highway and I..." I trail off, kicking at the dry ground, sending a small cloud of dust around my feet. Sweat beads along my brow and runs down my back, my clothes sticking to me. It's uncomfortable, but nowhere near as uncomfortable as the next words feel coming out of my mouth. "I need help."

"Where are you?"

I glance around, seeking out some sort of landmark I can describe for him. My eyes land on an old sign down the highway, barely close enough for me to make out. "I'm just outside of town on Highway 77. I can see the city limits sign from where I'm standing."

"You're *outside* of town."

"Yes."

I know what he's thinking: I left town without talking to him, without *consulting* him, something he's told me before is completely against the rules. But his rules are really more like wishes, and I know better than anyone that wishing is for fools. He can't scold me for something I'm not obligated to do, but the frustration in his voice is enough punishment.

I hate feeling like a disappointment.

"Got it," he says. "I'll send someone."

"Thank you," I whisper, but he's already hung up before I get the words out. Snapping the phone closed, I toss it onto the passenger seat through the open car door. My eyes drift back toward the sign down the highway, reading the white writing standing out against the grungy green paint.

Entering
SNOWFLAKE

It's an oxymoron, really, one I don't find any humor in. A town in the sweltering state of Arizona, not far from the Painted Desert, ironically named Snowflake.

This isn't my home.

Home is somewhere else, somewhere far, far away from this hellhole.

The sound of tapping glass echoed around me, rousing me from my light slumber. I blinked away the sleep, trying to adjust my eyes. The apartment was dark, the only light from the glimmer of the moon streaming in from outside, the soft glow splayed out along the wooden floor. I lay on the couch, staring straight ahead, watching as shadows dance along the living room walls.

It was quiet... *too* quiet... until I heard it again. The windowpane rattled behind me as the tapping once more reached my ears, sending my heart feverishly racing. Sitting up, I carefully peeked over, my eyes instantly meeting *his* — green eyes that shone so bright they were damn near the color of emeralds.

Instead of calming my heart, the sight of him sent my pulse racing more.

He stopped tapping when he noticed me looking, instead curving his pointer finger and beckoning me to come to him. Jumping up, I tiptoed over to the window, holding my breath as I shoved it open. It groaned, and creaked, like nails on a chalkboard, making me cringe.

He, on the other hand, just shook his head. "Way to be quiet, Gracie."

I could feel my face heating, and I knew the blush was visible thanks to my pale skin. I hoped he thought it was from the warmth and not because of him, but the twinkle in his eyes told me he was on to me.

He had always been on to me, honestly, ever since we were little kids.

"What are you doing here?" I asked incredulously as he crouched on the metal fifth floor fire escape outside my apartment window, like him being up here was the most normal thing in the world.

He shrugged. "I wanted to see you."

"You scaled a fire escape in the middle of the night because you wanted to see me?"

"Yes."

"How very *West Side Story* of you."

"Yeah, well, just don't expect me to start singing."

I knelt down on the floor and leaned against the old windowsill as I regarded him curiously. *Cody Moran.* Shaggy brown hair and fair skin and the brightest eyes I had ever seen. A scar marred the left side of his face, running from the corner of his mouth down along his chin.

It made him look a lot harsher than he ever had it in him to be.

He had the kind of smile that could knock the breath right out of you, the kind of smile that left you speechless, a weapon that could disarm even the strongest person once he unleashed it. It was a smile he rarely used, though, except for when he was alone with me.

Only me.

Slightly crooked, one dimple deeper than the other, one corner of his mouth not wanting to cooperate, like it held secrets it wasn't yet ready to spill. Some people might have called it a sinister smile, like he was somebody's conniving villain, but it brought me to my knees whenever I saw it.

Reaching through the open window, Cody grabbed the back of my neck and pulled me toward him without another word, like he could read my mind and knew I was thinking about his mouth. I leaned forward, my eyes drifting closed when his lips met mine. His were chapped but somehow still soft, his kiss sweeter than he looked capable of being. A bitter hint of alcohol lingered on his tongue, mixing with the flavor of spearmint from his gum.

He took his time, never deepening the kiss, holding me there with his grip, before finally pulling back. He left a trail of pecks near the corner of my mouth before letting go, laughing under his breath. "*So* worth hauling my ass up here for."

With that, he was gone.

The fire escape shook, the metal violently rattling as he carelessly took the steps two at a time. I opened my eyes and craned my neck to watch, leaning out the window in just enough time to see him fearlessly leap over a railing on his way back down.

I was grinning like a fool, watching the reckless boy.

God, I loved him.

"Grace."

The stern voice behind me sent me into a sudden panic. I jumped, startled, and misjudged how much room I had.

BAM

The back of my head banged against the window, shooting sharp pain through my skull and forcing tears to my eyes. I grimaced, pulling myself back into the apartment as I grabbed my throbbing head. "Shit."

The curse slipped from my lips and hung in the air around me, squeezing all the oxygen from the room. *Shit.* Shit was right. My watery eyes peeked across the dark living room, coming face-to-face with my father.

He stood in the doorway to the apartment, the front door wide open with his hand still grasping the knob. He was dressed casually, as usual, but his expression was perpetually stern. His hair was light colored, sort of long around the sides. He looked a bit like a guy from the old west. He even carried a Colt revolver tucked away somewhere, except... you know... he wasn't what I'd call a cowboy.

"Uh, Dad, hey." I rubbed my scalp, damn surprised that it wasn't bleeding considering hard as I banged it. "I didn't hear you come home."

"That's because the place was wide open," he said. "What did I tell you about locking doors, Grace?"

"To always do it."

"Exactly," he said. "So why wasn't this door locked?"

I had no excuse, except that I forgot, but I knew that answer wouldn't fly with my father, so I didn't bother saying anything at all.

He stared at me skeptically as he closed the front door, making a point to lock it before addressing me again. "What are you doing over there?"

"Just, uh, sitting here," I said, looking down at myself. *Yep, still kneeling on the floor.* "I was hot, you know... it's warm in here... so I thought I'd get some air."

I hoped that would explain the flush on my cheeks if he noticed it, but I was a terrible liar. Always had been. I couldn't fool anybody.

His expression clouded with suspicion as he strutted across the apartment, keeping his gaze fixed on my face until he was right beside me. His eyes flickered past me then, out of the open window, studiously scanning the fire escape before drifting toward the sidewalk. I glanced out, spotting Cody right away as he jogged across the busy street to where a group of boys were gathered on the corner. One of them playfully shoved Cody as soon as he reached them before pulling him into a headlock. Cody sucker punched him, breaking free from the grip, as another boy lit something and took a drag from it before passing it over to Cody.

From up there, the glowing embers looked just like a cigarette as he inhaled deeply, but I knew it wasn't. Cody had vices, and he certainly wasn't perfect. Not even close. He smoked weed and fought and didn't listen to *anybody*, but there was more good to him than there was bad. I had known him for as long as I had been breathing, and in that time, I saw the heart he tried to conceal.

It was the things he did when he thought nobody was watching—generously tipping, picking up litter, trapping spiders instead of killing them—that truly made him who he was, but I sometimes thought I was the only one who saw them… the only one who really saw *him*. Everyone else saw the boy with the filthy mouth and a tongue he didn't quite know how to hold… the boy with the bloodshot eyes and the constant scowl. The truth is, he was soft, and sweet, and compassionate… he just wore armor over all of it, armor meant to shield his sensitivity.

He had no choice.

He had to do it.

As the only son of Cormac Moran, notorious

leader of the largest Irish gang to ever run the streets of Manhattan, Cody had no choice but to put up walls of protection around him. In these streets, children often paid for their parent's sins, and he was no exception.

I watched as Cody blew a puff of smoke, releasing it from his lungs, before passing the joint on to another guy. The group started to leave, to walk away, but Cody hesitated on the corner and glanced back my direction. He didn't acknowledge me—I didn't know if he could really even see up there—but I could feel his gaze burn through me, anyway.

My father reached over then, not even pretending to be delicate as he slammed the window shut. He turned the squeaky old lock on top, securing it. "He's too old for you, Grace."

"He's only eighteen."

"And you're sixteen."

"And a half," I clarified. "Sixteen and a half."

"Ah, yes, *and a half.*"

His voice was borderline mocking as he stood there, staring down at me. His suspicious eyes had an edge to them as he clenched his jaw, like he was fighting the urge to say something more.

Something we both knew I wouldn't agree with.

Saying anything else about Cody was a waste of breath.

"Get some sleep, Grace," he decided on before turning to walk away. "Get a fan if you're hot, but don't open that window. It's not safe."

Twenty minutes pass—maybe less, maybe more—but it feels like an eternity, my entire body soaked with sweat, every inch of my fair skin tinged pink from the scorching sunshine, before a tow truck comes roaring down the highway. It pulls right up to my defunct car, the engine rumbling as the driver jumps out and ambles toward me. He's a big guy, about as round as he is tall, wearing coveralls and a tattered baseball cap. His beady eyes zero in on me like the scope of a sniper's rifle. I can practically see the red dot bouncing around my breasts. *Creep.*

I cross my arms over my chest, glaring at him, but I say nothing about his ogling. I wonder what he'd think if he knew the real me, if he'd be gawking at me like that if he knew the truth. If he knew I wasn't this shy girl without a voice. If he knew I'd been raised in a world where we didn't take shit from anybody.

"So I got a call about—"

I don't let him finish, don't pay his words any attention as I turn away, reaching into the car to grab what I need to salvage before slamming the door and brushing past him. I don't wait for an invitation, walking right over to his truck and climbing into the passenger seat, waiting in silence for him to do whatever it is he does.

He shrugs off my dismissiveness, grumbling something about a 'stuck up little bitch' as he sets to work. A year ago those words would've bothered me, but now?

14

Maybe that's just who this girl is.

He gets my car hooked up to tow it and climbs in beside me, saying nothing else as he pulls out onto the highway. He must've already been given all of the information because he doesn't ask me for an address, doesn't inquire about where he's supposed to take me. The man drives through quiet Snowflake, heading right down Main Street, passing only a handful of cars along the way. Although it's just the beginning of December, the town has been decorated for Christmas for weeks, big red bows affixed to all of the streetlights, lights on most of the businesses.

It's about a ten-mile drive to the little corner of nowhere where I live, isolated even in isolation, the small two bedroom house surrounded by abandoned, useless acres of desert land. The driver pulls right up to the house and turns to me, addressing me for the second time during this excursion.

"Your fella already paid," he grumbles. "Used a credit card when he called about you, so we're all squared away."

I nod, glad that my sunglasses conceal my eyes when I roll them at the word *'fella'*. It certainly wasn't my fella that called, but I don't correct him. It's probably better if he just thinks that, anyway. Getting out of the tow truck, I head for the house, leaving the man alone out in the front yard with my car, not telling him what to do with it.

He can have the piece of shit for all I care.

The house is expectedly quiet, and empty, but what I don't anticipate is for it to be so goddamn *stifling*. The air is hot and hazy, at least a few degrees hotter than outside, even without the sun's rays shining on the place.

Groaning, I toss my things down on the splintered wooden coffee table before heading for the controls for the central air. I press buttons, turning the thing off and back on again, dropping the temperature down a few degrees, hoping it'll kick on, but nothing happens.

"Great," I grumble. "Just what I need today."

Giving up, I open every window I can manage to pry open and start striping, leaving a trail of clothes from the living room to the only bathroom in the house. I turn the water on cold, starting the spray for the shower, and climb beneath it, leaning against the tile and just letting the coldness soothe my skin.

When I get out, the sun is starting to set outside. The tow truck is gone, my car parked right near the front door of the house. I throw on another pair of shorts and a tank top, twisting my wet hair up into my signature messy bun, not bothering to even brush it. I stop by the kitchen and search through the mostly empty refrigerator, finding little more than a six-pack of Guinness and some questionable leftovers.

I grab the beer.

It's too hot to eat anything, anyway.

I haven't had an appetite in days.

Plopping down on the old, threadbare couch in the living room, I kick my feet up on the coffee table and drink—one after another, until my body is tingly and my mind is fuzzy and I give up on pretending to be this miserable girl for the time being.

"The sausage is bangin'."

I was taking a sip of fresh hot coffee when Cody slipped right into the booth across from me. No hello, no nice to see you, no other greeting... nothing except for those words.

The sausage is bangin'.

"The sausage," I repeated, "is bangin'?"

He reached over and grabbed the fork from in front of me, stabbing a sausage link from my plate to take a bite of it. Chewing, he nodded, making a point to swallow before he said, "*definitely* bangin'."

Shaking my head, I took another sip from my cup. "Nice to know."

"You want a bite?" he asked, waving the fork toward me as he raised his eyebrows.

"No, thanks."

"Come on," he said. "You don't want my sausage?"

"Technically, it's *my* sausage," I pointed out. "And no, I'll pass on... you know..."

"My sausage," he said again, deliberately, as he stared across the table at me. Blush warmed my cheeks at the blatant innuendo. After a moment, his lips started to curve with a smile. It was barely there, but I saw it, the sight only making my blush run rampant. *Stupid boy and his stupid disarming smiles.* He let out a little laugh at my reaction. "You're missing out, you know. It's bangin'."

Rolling my eyes, I focused on my drink, taking

small sips as I watched him take another bite. He had no qualms reaching over eventually and just grabbing my whole plate, pulling it to him to finish what I didn't eat. That would probably annoy some people, maybe *most* people, but not me.

I found it amusing.

It was nice to see him act like a typical, obnoxious teenage boy sometimes.

I knew he wouldn't have hijacked my breakfast if he thought I was still hungry.

It was early in the morning on a Sunday. We hadn't planned to meet here, we never really did, but he always seemed to know where to find me. He always seemed to know when I was feeling lonely, when I could use his company. I never had to tell him.

He just knew.

I woke up that morning to an empty apartment. Nothing new in my life. My father was usually gone all hours of the night and most weekends, off doing God knows what God knows where with God knows who, leaving me to fend for myself. He left plenty of money, sure, but money couldn't buy everything. It didn't give me time or attention, love or affection. Money bought me breakfast there at the diner on the corner, but it was always this boy who supplied the rest of it.

Cody devoured what was left of the food, which was quite a bit. I wasn't really hungry to begin with. He ate it like he hadn't eaten in a week, which was absurd, because he was a spoiled little twit when it came down to it. Anytime he was hungry, all he had

18

to do was say the word and his mother would make him a four-course meal.

"So I'm guessing the old man didn't come home again."

I shook my head. "Nope."

"Yeah, Cormac decided not to grace us with his presence at breakfast this morning, either."

It always threw me off, even after years of hearing it, when he called his father by his first name. I regarded him curiously as I considered that, his actual words not sinking in for a moment. "Wait... *breakfast*? Does that mean you've already eaten this morning?"

"Of course."

Reaching over, I snatched my plate back away, my expression making him laugh. In turn, he stole the cup from my hand and brought it to his lips, taking a drink. Grimacing, he quickly set it back down and shoved it toward me. "I don't know how the hell you stomach that shit, Gracie."

Shrugging, I picked it right back up. "It's good."

"Coffee's only good when it's got Bailey's in it," he said, pointing the fork at me. "Add a little Irish Cream and we're in business."

"I'm not old enough for alcohol."

"Not old enough for coffee, either, if you ask me," he countered, "but that doesn't stop you from drinking it."

"There's no law against drinking coffee at my age."

He lounged in the booth, draping his arm over the back of it as he raised his eyebrows. "Bucking

19

family tradition and being a law-abiding citizen, are we?"

If I hadn't loved my coffee so much, I'd have thrown the cup right at him. But being as I *did* love it, I merely took another drink. He liked to tease me. I liked to act annoyed, but we both knew I got a thrill out of it. I never saw his playful side with anybody except me. I brought it out of him.

"More like my father would have my ass if he caught me drinking."

"Yeah," he agreed. "Conner always was a hypocritical bastard."

I didn't bother jumping to my father's defense when Cody said that. I didn't even get offended. If anything, I agreed with him. My father was never the *practice what you preach* type. He was always more the *do as I say and not as I do* kind of guy. Double standards were a way of life living under his roof.

A year and a half, I told myself. Eighteen more months until I was an adult, and then he couldn't stop me from living the way *I* wanted.

Cody and I sat in silence after that. It wasn't uncomfortable, not in the least, and I certainly didn't feel lonely anymore with him across from me. We always seemed to have that sort of connection—even as little kids, before hormones made everything tricky—where just being in the same place, at the same time, comforted us. We wouldn't even have to speak, or touch. Just breathing the same air did the trick.

I sipped my coffee, finishing what was left of it, and watched Cody as he stared out the diner

20

window. I wondered what he was thinking about, but I didn't ask. I knew he would tell me if he wanted to talk about whatever was on his mind.

The waitress brought my check, slipping it on the table. Before I could even reach for it, it was already in Cody's hand. He pulled some cash from his pocket, dropping a fifty-dollar bill beside my plate. I'd eaten here so much I knew my breakfast cost just shy of eleven bucks.

I followed him out of the diner. The moment we stepped out onto the sidewalk, Cody slipped his hand into mine. As we strolled down the block, his thumb gently stroked my skin, the movement so subtle I could barely feel it.

My apartment was across the street, only a few buildings away. It was barely a minute walk. Cody paused outside of my building and looked up at it, squinting from the sun, before he looked back at me. Silence surrounded us for another minute as we just stood there, holding hands. Even after knowing him for so many years, Cody had never been inside my apartment. He wasn't allowed. One of my father's many rules, but it had nothing to do with what he was packing in his pants.

I just wasn't allowed company. *Ever.*

No birthday parties, no sleepovers, no visiting friends.

It's not safe, my father said. *You don't leave your home open to anyone. You just can't.*

"I'll check back by later," Cody said. "You know, make sure he makes it home, so you're not alone."

"You don't have to."

21

"I know," he said, "but I will."

He leaned down, kissing me. It was barely a peck, a brush of his lips against mine, before he pulled away. He was never one for public displays of affection. Couldn't let them see past his armor and into his chest, lest they might realize Cormac Moran's boy was full of weaknesses.

He took a step back, his hand slipping from mine. I mourned the loss right away.

He said nothing else, motioning toward my building with his head.

I turned away from him and went inside, making my way up the flights of stairs to my apartment. I unlocked the door and stepped inside, remembering to relock it behind me, before strolling through the living room to the window. I glanced out, my eyes drifting down to the sidewalk, instantly seeing Cody.

He was still standing there, watching my window.

He saw me, and nodded, before strolling away.

I watched him leave, when everything inside of me didn't want him to go.

Darkness has completely fallen over Snowflake by the time I reach the last beer in my six-pack of Guinness. I pull the top off with my bottle opener when I see headlights flashing outside the open living room window, the familiar sound of tires against the dry, cracked earth as a car approaches the house. I listen as the engine shuts off, listen as someone gets out of the parked vehicle.

Seconds later, there's a tapping on the front door.

"It's open," I call out without bothering to get up, taking a sip of the warm Irish stout. I hate the taste of Guinness, but I'm not drinking it for the flavor. It does exactly what it's meant to do.

The door opens, the familiar voice carrying through right away. "The door's open, but it *shouldn't* be."

I stare at the doorway as he appears. He's easy to make out, even in the darkness, with his sturdy, statuesque body and bright blond hair. Always clean-shaven and dressed impeccably, he somehow still has an air of effortlessness surrounding him. He's a hard ass, all right, but he's the kind of hard ass that makes you feel at ease yielding to him. He's smart, and brave, and he's handsome, I suppose, if you like that sort of thing.

That sort of thing being forty year olds who are certified assholes for a living.

Holden.

Holden pauses just a foot inside the living room and stares at me. I can't make out much of his expression, his face cast in shadows, but I see enough to detect the exhaustion. His dark suit is ruffled, I assume from traveling, since he high-tailed his ass here after I called him this afternoon from the highway, but he still seems composed. His tie is the color of fresh blood, and over top of it, covering most of it, on a silver chain, hangs a badge.

A star with an eagle inside of it, wrapped in a

circle, *United States Marshal* written around it in bright blue. My eyes focus in on it as the metal gleams in the little bit of light streaming inside the house... anything to avoid looking him in the face.

I wish I were still wearing my sunglasses so he couldn't look me in the eyes.

Holden slowly strolls toward me, generous enough to not turn on any of the lights along the way. "What country are we in?"

"The great ol' U-S-of-A," I say. "The land of the free and the home of the brave."

"And the drinking age in America is...?"

"Twenty-one."

"And you are...?"

"Not twenty-one."

"That's what I thought."

He shoves my legs over to sit down on the coffee table in front of me. I'm damn surprised the piece of shit wood doesn't buckle under his weight. I tear my gaze away from the flashy badge and hazard a look at his face, finding exactly what I didn't want to see. Frustration. Disappointment. Pity. The whole gauntlet of pathetic emotions reflect right at me, making me feel more like a pesky little kid instead of my hard fought seventeen and nine-tenths. That look makes me feel like *this* girl, the one I'm not, the one he needs me to be... the one I've tried to be.

The one I just can't be.

I take a sip of the Guinness before holding it out to him. He hesitates, staring at it, before taking it from my hand. I'm surprised when he actually brings the bottle to his lips and takes a drink, knowing damn well he has as much business drinking right now as I do.

He grimaces, making a disgusted face as he swallows, but he doesn't put the beer down. He doesn't hand it back, either. Instead, he clutches the bottle with both hands between his legs as he stares at me.

He doesn't ask how I acquired the beer.

I'm glad, because then I'd feel inclined to admit I stole it, and I'm not in the mood for one of his *'there are certain things you just can't do'* lectures.

"Gracie, Gracie, Gracie..." His voice is quiet. "Talk to me."

I look away from him, unsure of what to say. His gaze is so intense that it's like being under an interrogation light. I practically feel myself start to sweat again. "The air conditioner is broken."

"Huh," he says. "I thought it felt hot in here."

"I came home tonight and it wasn't working. I tried turning it off and back on again, but it didn't work. I didn't know what else to do."

"Why didn't you call me?"

"Because I'd already called you about the car," I say. "I can't just call you every single time something goes wrong in my life. We'd never get off the phone if that was the case."

He laughs, but there isn't much humor to the sound. "That's what I'm here for."

Holden forces down the rest of the beer—I think simply to keep *me* from drinking it—before he stands up and starts gathering the empty bottles. He heads to the kitchen to throw them away. I wonder if he

25

ever gets sick of cleaning up other people's messes. That's all the man ever seems to do. I hear him looking around the sparse cabinets, see the light as he investigates the refrigerator. He returns after a minute, sitting back down in front of me.

"You have nothing to eat here."

"I'm not really hungry."

"But you have to eat sometime."

I shrug.

"I'll see about getting you a new car... a better car," he says. "In the meantime, we'll work on making some repairs around this place, and we'll restock the kitchen, because I can't have you starving on me here. Sound good?"

"Sure," I say. "Whatever."

My response isn't what he wants to hear. He sighs loudly, nudging my leg with his knee to try to get my attention. Humoring him, I glance his way, knowing he won't drop this until I do.

His expression is serious. "I'm worried about you, Gracie. Talk to me. Please. Tell me what's bothering you."

"I just... I feel like I'm suffocating."

"I promise we're going to get the air going again in here."

"No, I mean..." I hesitate, unsure of how to explain it, wondering if it'll even make a difference. *Probably not.* My opinion meant nothing growing up and it somehow means even less now. "I feel like I'm losing myself. Like really losing what makes me *me*. This house... this town... this life... it's not who I am."

"Tell me what will help," he says. "What will

make you happy?"

"Snow."

The word is involuntary as it slips from my lips.

Holden laughs, a hint of genuine amusement this time. He thinks I'm being sarcastic. He doesn't understand. He *can't*. "Well, I'll have you know, it actually snows in this part of Arizona. You just haven't lived here long enough to see it."

"But it's not just snow. It's all of it. It's cold mornings and hot coffee. It's bright lights and loud neighbors and sitting on a fire escape and taking in all of the commotion. It's makeup and dress shoes and nice clothes and a reason to wear all of it. It's my life. Mine. Not *this* girl's."

I motion toward myself to make my point. I'm surprised when, instead of more frustration, he offers a small smile of understanding. "I get it."

"Do you?"

"Yes," he says. "It would be dishonest to say I know *exactly* how you feel, because I haven't walked in your shoes before, but I get it. You're not the first person to feel this way. And I can promise it'll get better. With time, you'll get used to it."

"But I shouldn't have to," I say. "I shouldn't have to *get used to it*. It's not fair."

"It's not," he agrees. "But there's always an adjustment period. I've told you that before. You just need to give it a chance. Make friends… watch TV… get a hobby. Do *something* to pass the time. And I'm here any time you need anything. All you have to do is call. I'm not going anywhere. I promise. It's my job."

He says the last part with a smile, like it's meant

to ease my worries, but it only makes everything so much worse.

Holden isn't my friend.

He isn't my family.

Holden is my *handler*.

I can count on one hand how many people in the world know where I am at this moment, and every single one of them wears a U.S. Marshals Service badge. Out of them, Holden is the only one who has any personal contact with me. They're tight-lipped, even within their own department, their security stronger than a virgin locked up in a chastity belt. Holden deals with the person behind the name. To the others, I'm just paperwork.

That's the saddest part of all, I think. I have one person in the world... one person I can turn to, one person I can call for help these days, one person who can listen to me, one person to understand, and he's only there because he gets paid to be.

It's nothing like I had before.

I had love, and compassion, someone to turn to when my world turned cold.

This girl... she has nothing.

The familiar black town car pulled right up to the curb in front of the apartment building. I'd seen it hundreds of times before, navigating these streets over the years, always driven by Cormac Moran. It parked, the engine still idling based on the smoke coming from the exhaust, but nobody got out of the thing.

I stared down at it, the evening breeze ruffling my hair, blowing tendrils into my face. I brushed them away, tucking the soft red curls behind my ears. It was just after dusk and the air was cool, summer having faded away much too quickly.

I was sitting cross-legged on the fire escape, the cold metal pressing into my thighs. My heels were abandoned on the other side of the open window, discarded on the living room floor when I realized I wouldn't need them today.

A few minutes passed before the passenger door to the car finally opened and someone stepped out. I recognized my father right away. He shut the door and stood along the curb as the car whipped back into traffic and sped away.

Once it was gone, my father's shoulders slumped, his poised posture fading. It was as if he'd just let out a deep breath he'd been holding for a long time. Even from five stories up, I could sense his exhaustion. For as long as I could remember, he always seemed drained, like he had little left to offer anyone... especially me. He had nothing for me, it seemed.

After running his hands down his face, he turned and stalked toward the building, disappearing from my view. A minute later I heard the front door unlocking, footsteps echoing through the apartment.

"Grace?"

I didn't respond, my eyes focused on my feet. My pantyhose were ripped from getting caught on some jagged metal on the fire escape, a line running the whole way down my left leg to my foot. My toenails were painted red to match my new dress. *What a waste of effort.*

"Grace!"

His voice had a panicked edge to it, his footsteps harder along the wooden floor. He seemed to be doing circles, checking all the rooms, before coming to an abrupt halt right by the window. I didn't turn to look, but I could sense his intense gaze.

He spotted me.

He shoved the window up further to come through, perching himself on the windowsill. He sighed exasperatedly, clasping his hands together in front of him as he propped his elbows on his knees.

"I forgot."

I forgot. He said those words like they were supposed to fix this, like they would make it better and not worse instead.

He forgot.

How the hell could he forget?

Ten years had passed since my mother died. I had been so young back then that I was starting to forget so much—the feel of her hugs, the sound of her laughter, the way she spoke my name—but I'd never forget *her.*

I'd never forget today.

I could feel tears in my eyes, and I blinked them back, grateful none escaped. I didn't want to ruin my makeup. I spent a long time doing it.

"I got busy," he continued. "I didn't mean to forget. It just slipped my mind."

We were supposed to go see her.

She was buried out in Queens.

We went every year on the anniversary.

Not this year.

"Look, I'm exhausted. It's been a long week and I'd like to get some sleep and forget any of this happened. I'm just so tired of all of it. I'm ready to forget."

I wasn't sure what to say.

He knew I wouldn't say anything.

Climbing back into the apartment, he paused. "It's not safe for you out here, especially after dark. I've told you before about leaving that window open."

He didn't wait for me to come back inside before walking away, heading off to his bedroom. He knew I'd obey him.

Eventually.

The sky grew darker, but the neighborhood was as alive as ever. After nightfall was when the hellions really came out to play. I watched them, recognizing so many faces, even seeing Cormac drive by again, rushing off to do whatever the man did. Nobody noticed me up there, though.

Nobody ever looked.

Nobody but *him.*

Cody was out with his friends. Most of them lived a few blocks up, Cody included, but they tended to hang out down here instead. It was because of me, he once said. The other boys followed Cody's lead, and he gravitated here to be near me. Even when we couldn't be together, he took solace in the fact that I wasn't far away.

I spotted the group on the corner across the street,

smoking and roughhousing near the diner as usual. I watched him for a few minutes before he glanced my way, spotting me sitting up there. He broke away from his friends then, passing the joint off to one of the others, and exhaled a puff of smoke.

"Grace!" my father shouted from in the apartment. "Inside. *Now.*"

Something got into me then.

Something struck me in that moment.

I didn't care if it would bring me trouble... I needed him.

I needed Cody.

The next thing I knew, I was on my feet, but instead of slipping back into the window and following my father's demands, I was moving away from it. Cody jogged across the street, pausing in front of my building, his brow furrowing when he saw me. I navigated the fire escape, not as easily as he always did it. When I reached the bottom, he grabbed the ladder, pulling it down to help me.

The moment my feet hit the filthy sidewalk, I launched myself at him. Cody stiffened, caught off guard. "Whoa, whoa, whoa... what's wrong, love?"

The dam broke unexpectedly. Tears flooded my cheeks. I couldn't speak. Cody wrapped his arms around me, one arm clutching me tightly while his right hand made its way into my hair, grasping the back of my head and holding me against his chest as I sobbed.

"It's going to be okay," he said quietly. "Whatever it is, whatever happened... it's going to be okay. I promise it."

Never once did he try to shush me.

Never did he tell me not to cry.

He held me, standing on the sidewalk, ignoring the looks from passersby, and let me get it out. My tears slowed eventually and I caught my breath, but he still wouldn't let go of me.

"I'm sorry," I whispered, nearly choking on the words. This right here wasn't Cody. He didn't like people knowing his business, and I was making one hell of a scene.

"Don't apologize," he said. "I'm always here for you, Gracie. *Always.*"

Those words brought on a fresh round of tears, but I got myself back under control quickly, pulling myself together enough to pull away from him. I hated myself for falling apart, embarrassed by my losing it, but Cody merely looked at me with worry—not because of me, but *for* me.

He worried about me.

Reaching over, he cradled my face in his hands, his thumbs brushing the tears from my cheeks. Black smears from my mascara smudged his skin as he wiped it all away.

"The bastard forgot what today was, didn't he?"

Slowly, I nodded. Cody's scowl deepened. He pulled me right back into his arms. I didn't cry anymore, but he continued to hug me.

It felt like an eternity.

Goose bumps coated my skin.

I pulled away eventually, knowing I needed to get back upstairs before I got caught down here with him, seeing Cody's friends were watching us curiously, waiting for him to join them again. They knew about us, of course... the whole neighborhood knew. We'd never been a secret, but we tried to never make a spectacle out of it.

I tried to point that out, but he interrupted my thought process.

"You look beautiful today, Gracie."

Those words stalled me. "I'm a mess."

He shook his head. "You're always beautiful, but I like your hair when you wear it down like that. The curls, you know... I dig that shit."

I smiled softly. "Thank you."

Thank you for trying to make me feel better about the fact that I have raccoon eyes and I'm running around in ripped pantyhose and no shoes.

He stared at me for a moment before leaning closer, his expression serious. He knew I didn't believe him. "I mean it. You're fucking beautiful. When you're laughing, when you're crying, and every moment in between. There's *nobody* more beautiful to me. And don't ever apologize for what just happened. When you hurt, I hurt. You don't ever have to go through that alone, Gracie."

I nodded, and he did the same, before he grabbed the ladder for the fire escape, tugging it back down. I started for it, but he stopped me long enough to kiss my still-damp cheek.

"You remembered," he whispered. "That's all that matters. Fuck him."

Twelve months.

I've been this new girl for almost exactly a year now, and it has yet to get any easier for me. I had just turned seventeen when the Marshals showed up in the middle of the afternoon, telling me everything in my world was about to change. It was an abrupt decision, one that I certainly didn't see coming... one that would alter my life *forever*.

Witness Protection.

The first few weeks were pure hell.

I was taken straight from my apartment in the Hell's Kitchen neighborhood of Manhattan to a secure location outside of Washington to debrief, where I was isolated and put on lockdown. You see, being as I was a minor, I was supposed to have a guardian with me in the program, but I came in alone.

It begged the question: What to do with me?

At the beginning, I was practically imprisoned, always guarded and not allowed to roam, until Holden put his foot down, stepping up to accept responsibility. I was old enough, and mature enough, he said, to live somewhere by myself. After all, I'd practically been doing it for years. I was allowed to pick my new last name—Gracie Callaghan traded in for the equally Irish yet sort of pretentious sounding Grace Kennedy—but Holden picked the less than glamorous location.

Snowflake.

At the beginning, Holden visited every day, staying for hours, calling multiple times to check in. But as the months wore on, the visits became less frequent. Now I see him for a few minutes once a week, if that.

He has others, I figure.

Others he needs to keep an eye on.

Other *responsibilities*.

As if on cue, Holden glances at his watch from where he's sitting on the coffee table in front of me, like he's worried he's already overstayed his time. "I should find a hotel for the night."

"You can just stay here," I say, motioning down the hallway behind me. "You know where the spare room is."

"I shouldn't," he says. "There are rules."

"Yeah, well, I'm pretty sure there are also rules against drinking and driving on the job."

Our situation has never exactly been by the book, so nothing was ever really set in stone about how he's supposed to deal with me. In general, inspectors and witnesses aren't supposed to fraternize, but it's kind of hard to keep things strictly business when he took the reins as my temporary guardian.

He stands up, but instead of heading for the door, he takes a step further into the living room, turning toward the hallway. He pauses there, staring down at me. "Why'd you cross out of the city limits this afternoon?"

I shrug. "Looking for a change of scenery, I guess."

He doesn't look like he buys my answer, but it's the truth.

"Get some rest, Gracie," he says. "Tomorrow will be a better day."

I offer him a smile in exchange for that piece of

shit advice, knowing he means well. He might even actually believe it. He reaches over and gently squeezes my shoulder in a silent sort of 'goodnight' gesture before making his way back to the guest bedroom.

I sit in silence once he's gone, staring at the clock on the wall in the darkness.

It's almost midnight.

Tomorrow doesn't look so promising.

My black comforter was spread out on the fire escape. I lay on my back on top of it, my knees pulled up, bare feet flat against the metal. Cody lies beside me, wedged against the railing. It wasn't very comfortable, trying to lay out here together, but neither of us complained.

Out loud, anyway.

His soft sighs of exasperation told me how he was feeling. The scowl on his face was deep tonight. Fall had come upon us quickly. I had to head back to school the following week—my junior year at the private all-girls catholic academy my father insisted on sending me to—while Cody started his senior year at a local high school. He should've graduated the year before, but a string of suspensions derailed that. He jumped from school to school, getting kicked out for fighting as soon as he got admitted, before having no option left but to resort back to public education.

Even then, they had a hard time finding one to

admit him. He would have to travel to Queens every morning for classes, which might turn out for the best, considering his reputation in *this* neighborhood.

"Do you ever wonder why they call it Hell's Kitchen?"

I wasn't sure what prompted the question as it flowed from my lips. I could hear the bustle of the neighborhood below us. Somewhere, in those streets, my father was running loose. So was Cody's, for that matter.

I didn't know what they were doing.

I wondered if Cody did.

"There's a story on the street," Cody said, "that it got its name because the neighborhood is the worst part of Hell... the *hottest* part. Hell's Kitchen. I don't know how true that is, but it sure as shit fits, considering Cormac runs the place."

I would've laughed, but I knew he wasn't joking.

"So does that make my father one of Satan's minions?"

"That's one way to put it."

"Is there any other way?"

He paused. "No."

I stared straight up in the sky, mulling over his words. Cormac had probably hundreds of followers. The police called them the *Hellions*, a nickname the younger generation embraced. My father, on the other hand, scoffed at it, calling it insulting. He had been around since the beginning, since the day Cormac took control of Hell's Kitchen. According to Cody, he was Cormac's right hand man.

It was a dark night, cloudless and cool. It was as if

a blanket of black lay above us, too. Sometimes, I thought, it was hard to feel grounded when you couldn't recognize the world around you. My eyes searched the skies, but I felt nothing spark inside of me. It was like we were trapped in a void. "You know, I can't remember the last time I saw a star."

"Me, either," Cody said. "I can't remember the last time I actually *looked* for one."

We lay there some more, and I knew we were both looking for stars, looking for something beyond this existence and out into the greater universe, but just like me, he came up empty. It sort of made it feel like this was all there was.

Like there was nothing outside of this life we had been given.

We both wanted more, though. Cody had told me, one of the secrets we shared in the dark on my sixteenth birthday, the first time he told me he had fallen in love with me and I whispered those words right back. He said he didn't want to be like his father... that he didn't want to waste his life running these streets.

He said he wanted out of Hell's Kitchen.

I said I wanted the same.

"I guess that does it," he said after a while. "Can't see the Heavens so this *must* be Hell."

"Must be," I mumbled in agreement, giving up on stargazing to snuggle up against him. I lay my head on his shoulder as he wrapped his arm around me. He smelled woodsy, and earthy, the pungent aroma of smoke lingering on his clothes and mixing with his cologne. Closing my eyes, I inhaled deeply, breathing him in.

He smelled like a world outside of this city.

He shifted position, cupping my chin and pulling my face up toward him so he could kiss me. It was soft and sweet as always, his tongue meeting mine as his hands roamed. He caressed my face and neck before his hand drifted down to my waist, toying with the hem of my shirt for a moment. I felt his fingertips graze the bare skin along my side as he dipped beneath the fabric. He stroked my stomach, moving up, his hand slipping beneath the cup of my bra, pushing it out of the way to palm my breast.

His thumb grazed across my nipple and I gasped, savoring his touch. This was what we did, the moments I lived for, when his hands were touching me, the only hands that *ever* touched me. It never went farther than this; he never pushed for more than just a stolen embrace.

His lips found my neck, kissing lightly, running his tongue along my skin.

I shivered.

"Are you cold?" he asked quietly.

I was, but that wasn't what gave me goose bumps right then. "I'm okay."

He sighed. "You should probably go in."

"I don't want to."

I didn't want him to leave.

I didn't want to spend another night by myself.

I was so tired of it.

I was only sixteen and three quarters and I was already drowning in solitude. I felt like I'd spent an entire lifetime alone. I didn't want to be alone anymore.

"Come with me," I whispered. "Lets go inside together."

He pulled away to look at me, surprise on his face as he stared into my eyes. He never went inside. It was just the way it was. Cody had broken every rule ever forced upon him, even broken a few laws in his young life, but this rule he followed. Maybe it was a matter of respect. Maybe it was fear.

Or maybe it was just because I'd never asked him to break it.

Maybe that was what he had been waiting for.

An invitation.

Because he gave it ten seconds then—ten seconds of silence, of contemplation—before he removed his hand from my shirt. I thought he was going to leave, that he was going to send me in alone. His expression was so serious.

It made my insides curl.

Cody motioned toward the open window. I climbed through, bringing my blanket with me as he got to his feet. I stood in the living room, straining my ears as he paused again. Ten more seconds. Ten seconds of silence. Ten seconds of contemplation. I listened for the sound of the rattling fire escape, expecting him to disappear. Instead, after those ten seconds passed, he came toward me, climbing through the window.

His feet hit the wooden floor, and something inside of me sparked, what I couldn't feel outside. Like we belonged...

He stood there, looking around. My place was nowhere near the size of his. The Morans lived in a fancy apartment in the newest building in the neighborhood, the kind of place without rusty old fire escapes and creaky windows.

For the first time in my life, standing in front of him, I was actually *nervous*.

I wringed my hands together, biting my bottom lip, unsure of what to say, or do, or what we were even doing anymore, but as usual Cody knew.

Cody always knew.

Reaching over, he grabbed my hands, stopping my anxious fidgeting. Wordlessly, he pulled me from the living room, leading me straight back to my bedroom, not even asking me which one it was. "How do you know—?"

"Just because I've never been inside doesn't mean I don't know the layout," he said. "I see your shadow moving around the apartment when you're alone."

From most people, that would probably sound creepy as fuck, but coming from him, it made my heart soar. He was always looking out for me, even when I didn't realize it.

My room was typical for someone my age, I supposed—clothes everywhere, shoes all over the floor. Shades of pink mixed with the darkest black, the walls covered in posters and things cut out of magazines. I didn't have movie stars or singers—no, I had places. Places I wanted to go. Things I want to see. My walls were a visual bucket list of dreams.

Cody's eyes scanned them in the darkness. It was all things he knew. I told him everything. But still, I was nervous.

Cody pulled me to him before I could start to

fidget again. "You have nothing to worry about. It's just me."

"I know."

"We don't have to do a thing."

Again, I knew, but I wanted to, and that was what made me nervous. I wrapped my arms around his neck, my fingers lacing through the messy hair at his nape as he kissed me. He didn't rush me, didn't push me, but he didn't force me to take the lead, either. Even though we both knew there was no reason for it, he could sense my anxiety. He pulled me over to my bed, laying me down on it. His hands roamed, slipping beneath fabric and exploring bare skin, as he kissed me.

And kissed me.

And kissed me some more.

He kissed me until I was breathless, until every inch of me was on fire from the inside out. My clothes were tugged off, one-by-one, discarded along with his shirt, until I was laying there in nothing but my underwear. My nerves intensified along with the rampant beat of my heart as his mouth traveled everywhere. Pleasure mingled with an edge of fear, adrenaline like never before coursing through my veins, making me tremble beneath him. His lips traveled down my chest, between my breasts, before trailing along my stomach. He moved along my sides, leaving kisses on my hips. I writhed, my hands running through his hair, as his tongue swirled around my navel before going lower...

Lower...

Lower...

43

He rubbed against me, teeth nipping around the black cotton of my underwear. Even with the fabric separating us, the spark of pleasure that rushed through me was intense. I arched my back, gasping, gripping tightly to his hair as his mouth explored that one place he had never been before. His hands grabbed the sides of my underwear, pulling them down, leaving me completely naked beneath him before I even had a chance to wrap my brain around the fact that this was actually happening. His gaze trailed along my body as he made his way back up, hovering over top of me. He met my eyes, a smile slowly overcoming his lips, wiping away that harsh scowl. Laugh lines and dimples nearly rendered his scar invisible.

He was so beautiful when he smiled.

I wished he'd do it more.

He kissed the corner of my mouth, his bare chest pressing against mine. I wondered if he could feel my heart beating, if he could hear it speed up even more when he unbuckled his pants. He took off the rest of his clothes, and I let my eyes explore. He was covered in battle scars—some from fighting, others his father put there—way too many scars for his eighteen years.

He seemed so at ease, so confident, not a stitch of nerves showing. I tried to always be strong like him, untouchable by outside forces, but he single-handedly disarmed me.

"Have you...?" My voice sounded magnified in the quiet bedroom. "Have you done this before?"

He paused again. Another ten seconds. It felt like ten years as he stared down at me, his smile suddenly gone. After those seconds pass, he seemed to find the words to speak. "You think I'd do this with somebody else, Gracie?"

Stupid question, because no, he wouldn't. We never had the kind of talk other people do, the kind of talks I heard the girls at school whispering about. It had just *always* been us, in a way. Just me and Cody. My best friend. My soul mate.

"I love you, Grace Elizabeth Callaghan," he said, his voice a serious whisper, like he was spilling a deadly secret that was far too big for the world to hear. "Nobody else. *Nobody*. Nobody else gets me. Nobody else can have me. I'm yours, as long as you want me, *if* you want me. Fuck knows, I don't know why you *would*, but if you do..."

I did.

I didn't say it, though.

It sounded like a silly declaration, the kind that words could never do justice. Instead, I pulled him back down to me, kissing him. He settled between my thighs, and my breath hitched when I feel him press against me.

"I'll try to be careful," he said. "I don't want to hurt you."

Slowly, he pushed in. I wouldn't have called it comfortable, but it wasn't painful. It was pressure, accompanied by a slight ache when he started to move. My muscles eased after a moment, my body relaxing as I started to adjust to the strange sensation of him being inside of me. I wrapped my arms around him as he covered my body with his own, sliding in and out, finding his rhythm. His lips found mine, never leaving, swallowing every moan and cry, every hitch of breath, knowing they were intended for him and him alone.

It was over too soon.

He stilled on top of me, breathing heavily. His forehead was pressed against mine. I opened my eyes, seeing his were closed, a relaxed expression on his face. A smile touched his lips again, natural and graceful. I didn't even know if he realized he was smiling.

I may not have seen any stars that night, but this couldn't really be Hell, I thought… not when I looked at him and swore I could see Heaven.

Witness Protection, or WITSEC, is nothing like the movies make it out to be. Like most people, my impression of it came from Hollywood storylines, but reality slapped me in the face the second I involuntarily joined.

There is no glitz, no exotic locales, no sitting on beaches sipping fruity drinks with tiny umbrellas as a generous gift of gratitude from the government for giving up your life. They legalized my new name with all of the proper documents, and shell out barely enough money every month to cover the bills for this rundown house, but other than that, I'm on my own. It's Holden's job to make sure I'm happy—I know, because he's told me that more than once. It's how I acquired the twenty-year-old broken down Chevy in the first place: the government's idea of going 'above and beyond'.

When I wake up the next morning, the first day of December, the air is still muggy. I'm sweating like a pig, my skin clammy and face flushed. I'm fucking miserable as I climb out of bed, not bothering to change clothes or even get dressed for the day.

It's not like I have any plans, anyway.

I roll up my shorts along the waistband, jacking them up even shorter, and bunch my tank top up in the front, tucking it into my bra to get it off my stomach. I don't give a shit how I look, nor do I care if it's inappropriate with present company… it's hot and all I want to do is stay cool.

Opening my bedroom door, the first thing I hear is noise in the kitchen, before the scent of food hits me like a freight train. My stomach instantly starts growling in response. Above that smell is something else, something I haven't smelled in a while. *Coffee.* Curious, I make my way that direction, pausing momentarily in the living room when I nearly trip over an air conditioner lying on the floor. It's one of those little window units, big enough to maybe cool half a room in this place.

I step around it, heading for the kitchen, spotting Holden standing in front of the stove, wielding a spatula. He's dressed, still looking composed even when going without a tie, his shirt sleeves rolled up to his elbows. He's not wearing his badge, probably because he's not supposed to around me.

We have this façade to maintain.

Cover stories are a bitch.

47

They drilled mine into me before I relocated here... Grace Kennedy, hailing from upstate New York, no relation to the actual Kennedy family if anyone got too nosey. I live with my uncle, who works in international trade, so he's gone more than he is at home. They even trained me to call him 'Uncle Holden', but it creeps me out to think of him like that. It's a simple story to pull off, not hard to remember, but I always feel like people can tell I'm bullshitting whenever I speak.

Holden, on the other hand, effortlessly lies. It's sort of awe-inspiring.

He'd make a good actor.

Or maybe one hell of a conman.

"Good morning, Grace," he says as he turns to face me, his voice coated with a phony New York accent that he somehow manages to make sound authentic. "I hope you're hungry."

I stare at him with confusion, wondering why he's speaking that way. He raises his eyebrows, subtly nodding toward the open window across the room. Glancing that way, I see a figure out in the yard, the hood up on my old car as a man tinkers with it. It's the same guy from yesterday, the tow truck driver who picked me up along the highway. The sight of him ties my stomach in knots. In public, I work hard to pretend to be this Grace Kennedy, the girl I'm not, but I relish on getting to be just Gracie again within the privacy of these walls.

As much of Gracie as I have left in me, anyway.

"Sure," I say. "Starving."

Holden smiles, knowing I've caught on, and

48

waves toward the small kitchen table with the spatula. "Have a seat."

I head for the refrigerator instead, curious, and find it packed full—he went shopping without me. Shaking my head, I sit down, just as he sets a cup of coffee on the table. I think it's meant for him but I snatch it for myself anyway, picking it up to blow in it. "You don't have any Bailey's to go in this, do you?"

He shoots me a look that tells me I'm out of my mind. Shrugging, I take a sip of the coffee and grimace, knowing he bought that generic bitter shit even *I* can barely stomach.

I watch in silence as he makes up a big plate of food and slaps it down on the table in front of me. He joins me with his own plate after a moment, as well as another cup of coffee, immediately diving into the food, while I just stare at mine. Holden's game is strong this morning. I'm almost impressed. He tried to replicate the traditional Irish breakfast: bacon, sausage, eggs, hashbrowns, and beans. While I appreciate the effort—really, I do—he should most definitely keep his day job. The bacon's not crispy, the hashbrowns are soggy, the eggs dried up and the beans... dear God, the beans came straight out of a Campbell's can.

I can sense him watching me as he devours his breakfast. I take a few bites to alleviate his concerns, but it doesn't seem to work. His expression slowly shifts, his worry again shining through.

"Not good?" he asks quietly, dropping his voice low to ensure only I can hear as he lets the accent slip. "I can find you something else to eat."

"It's fine," I say, giving him another smile, but he doesn't buy it.

His gaze bounces between our plates before he lets out a deep sigh. "Look, I know it's not perfect... frankly, I'm not Irish, nor am I what we'd call a good cook. I googled and thought I'd try to make you something special. You know, because it's your—"

Holden doesn't get a chance to finish what he's saying, and I'm grateful for it. His words are cut off by the loud bang of my car hood slamming closed. Seconds later, the engine of the Chevy roars to life, rumbling and hesitating, but it stays cranked.

Holden shoves his chair back and stands, walking out of the kitchen. I hear the front door open and set my fork down, watching out the window. Holden approaches the man, the two exchanging some words, Holden's New York accent back in full force. The car is turned back off and they shake hands, before Holden pulls out his wallet, handing over a big wad of cash to the man.

I turn back to my food, slouching down in my chair, but I don't eat any. Holden returns as the tow truck rumbles down the road, the man leaving, the job done. "So what happened to getting me a *new* car?"

Holden retakes his seat across from me. "That's still on the agenda, but it'll take some time for approval to come through."

I know that.

I do.

They're quick to pull you in, but once they have you, they start dragging their feet.

"And the air conditioning?"

"Same," he says. "I've got a window unit to install for the time being."

"Too swamped to fix the problems," I say, "yet they somehow found the chance to approve minor repairs."

Holden doesn't say anything, but he doesn't have to. I know it wasn't the government that paid for any of this. That money came right out of Holden's pocket.

"Call it a gift," he says after a moment.

"Friends give gifts. Family gives gifts. Handlers don't give gifts."

"I don't like that word."

"What? Handler?"

Holden cringes. "It insinuates you're something I need to handle."

"Aren't I?"

His eyes shoot daggers at me.

Maybe he doesn't think of me that way, I don't know, but that's how it feels. He does whatever he can to placate me, not realizing it usually just makes me feel worse. I'd rather be ignored than be humored. It's condescending.

Pushing my chair back, I stand up, picking up my breakfast. I scrape the food in the trashcan before tossing the plate in the empty sink and heading for the door. "Thanks for breakfast, Holden. I appreciate the effort."

Academy of Our Lady of the Sacred Heart. I never liked the name. I liked the school even less. I stood on the front steps after final dismissal my first day back, staring down at the sidewalk at the last person I expected to see standing in front of the ornate stone building.

My father.

He was wearing gray slacks and a white button down, the top few buttons undone. His hands were in his pockets, his gaze everywhere except for on me.

I almost wanted to run back inside before he saw me.

His presence tended to bring bad news. There was no reason for him to be there, which meant one of two things: either I was in trouble or else *he* was.

He scanned my classmates as they rushed past, laughing and chatting, paying him no mind. It was an unseasonably warm fall afternoon, so most of the girls were taking advantage of it, their skirts rolled up to indecent levels, shirts tied in knots, showing their midriff. But there I stood, the picture perfect Catholic schoolgirl: knee-high socks, gray plaid skirt, white shirt and gray blazer.

All I was missing were a pair of Mary Janes.

A bewildered look covered my father's face as he turned my way. He scanned me quickly, probably to ensure I didn't look like the rest of the girls around there. I descended the steps toward him, knowing I couldn't hide now.

"What happened to the dress code?"

"They don't get paid enough to enforce it."

"They're nuns, for Christ's sake," he grumbled.

"They're supposed to do it because the good book tells them to."

I didn't argue, but seeing as he probably knocked out every last commandment from his to-do list, he was the last person who ought to lodge a complaint about someone's holiness. He shook his head, meeting my eyes, but he said nothing else. He didn't look angry, at least. Maybe just exasperated.

"Is there, uh… is there a reason you're here?"

"Just wanted to see how your first day back was."

My brow furrowed. "You couldn't ask me that at home?"

"I had some free time so I thought I'd make up for what I missed. You know… thought we could go see your mother today."

I just stared at him as those words sunk in. It had been over a month since the anniversary, over a month since he *forgot*. I figured he just chalked it up to a loss, that it was time to move on, but this? This was even worse.

He was *just* now making time for me.

Just now making time for her.

I didn't argue, although I was scarcely in the mood to go. My father called for a car to drive us to Queens, right to the cemetery. My mother was buried in a family plot, a massive headstone adorning it that would someday also have my father's name on it.

It was nothing like it usually was.

Usually there were flowers, and tears, sometimes laughter and stories.

We were both quiet today.

Very little was spoken before we left again,

heading to a small restaurant around the corner, the same place we ate at every year on the anniversary. It was my mother's favorite. I couldn't remember that, but my father told me.

We both ordered meatloaf, also my mother's favorite.

Another thing I didn't remember.

He ate while I picked at my food, wanting to just go home and end this sham of an outing. Sometimes 'better late than never' was complete and utter bullshit.

"You know I love you, right, Grace?"

The question surprised me, not because he had to ask, but because he said that word: *love*. He said it less than Cody acknowledged Cormac as his father, which was practically never. Not to say I doubted my father's love. He loved me in his own way. I just always doubted his ability to express it normally. "Yes."

"You're everything I got that means something. I know you hate all these rules, but you're only sixteen…"

"And three quarters."

"And three quarters," he agreed, "but it's still not seventeen, and certainly not eighteen. It's my job to keep you safe, so that's what I do."

I heard it all before. My lack of friends, my not being allowed to go anywhere that isn't pre-approved… it was for the best, he claimed. *You don't need all that anyway.* But that was easy for him to say. Let him shove his feet in those ugly Mary Janes and walk a mile in the shoes of the girl he wanted me to be, and then let him come tell me she didn't need anything else.

"I want you to listen to me, and listen to me *good*," he said, a stern edge to his voice when I didn't respond to his declaration. "I'll do anything I have to... *anything*... to keep you out of trouble. And you aren't always going to like it, but it's not my job to cater to you. I gave you life. My only job is to make sure you stay living."

"Living," I muttered. "I think we define that differently."

"You're still breathing, aren't you? Still got enough breath in those lungs to complain, don't you? Then I'd say you're doing a lot more *living* than some others I know. These kids running the streets after dark, raising hell, smoking pot and hanging out on the corner, fighting and fucking off... they're not living, Grace. Those kids are just slowly dying. It's only a matter of time."

He was talking about Cody. He didn't have to use his name to get his point across. I continue to pick at my food, wishing he would finish, but no... Connor Callaghan was just getting started.

"That boy's a troublemaker," he said. "That's all he is."

My response was immediate. "So are you."

My father may not have been as notorious as Cormac, but he made quite a name for himself. He may have shielded me from most of what he did, but he couldn't hide the whole truth from me—not and still keep me safe.

"I do what I do for you, Grace. I'm not saying I'm

perfect, but I look out for you. Boys like him... they'll only bring you trouble. Even his father will tell you that. He's no good."

But he was, I thought.

He was good.

My father just couldn't see it.

He looked at Cody and saw a younger version of Cormac.

He looked at him and saw *himself*.

But Cody wasn't like his father, nor was he anything like mine, and nobody would ever convince me otherwise.

Throughout the rest of dinner, after paying the check, and on the entire drive home, my father went through it again, trying to pound it into my head that he knew what was best for me, and what was best for me wasn't anything I wanted. He had us dropped off down the block from the apartment building, and I grabbed my school bag, keeping my head down as we headed for home.

We were two buildings away when I heard the familiar voice. I looked up, catching sight of Cody across the street, hanging out with the same boys he usually hung with. He was talking to them but his eyes followed me. He saw me looking and brought his hand to his mouth, subtly kissing two of his fingertips before motioning my way.

My cheeks flushed at the acknowledgement.

Cody's eyes turned to my father then. He stared at him for a moment before turning away.

When we reached the apartment building, my father opened the door, but he didn't follow me inside. "Go upstairs. I'll be there in a minute."

He waited for me to listen before he walked away. I scaled the stairs faster than I'd ever taken them before, fumbling with the locks and rushing into the apartment, dropping my bag right inside the door. I ran over to the window, my heart racing when I looked out.

My father was already across the street, standing right in front of Cody.

His friends scattered. I wondered if my father scared them away. But Cody... Cody didn't look intimidated in the least. He stood there, hands in the pockets of his hoodie, shoulders relaxed, staring up at my father as he towered over him. It wasn't that Connor Callaghan was a big man, per se. It was just the way he carried himself, like he was invincible.

My father was talking. I didn't know what he was saying, but his lips were moving, and that alone was bad enough. Cody hadn't uttered a single word that I saw, merely staring at the man as he went on and on.

After a moment, Cody shook his head.

That was it.

Just a shake of the head to set my father off.

Anger clouded his expression as he took a step forward, going toe-to-toe, pointing his finger right in Cody's face as he screamed so loudly I could faintly hear his voice up on the fifth floor with the window closed. Cody tolerated the berating for a moment before taking a step back, and another, and another, before he paused to finally speak.

It was just a few words before he turned around and strolled away, leaving my father standing there

57

on the sidewalk alone, fuming.

I stepped away from the window when my father started toward the building again. Grabbing my school bag, I plopped down on the couch to do my homework, but I was too wound tight to focus.

I looked up when my father came in, slamming doors and throwing things. He wouldn't meet my eyes. "Go to your bedroom, Grace."

I obliged right away.

The man barely made a sound after that. Curiosity ate at me as time passed, one hour turning into the next, before there was a soft tapping on my bedroom door. It opened before I could acknowledge the knocking, and my father appeared. He changed his clothes. *Of course.* The sun had set, darkness cloaking the city, which meant he was off to work. "I'm heading out."

"Okay."

"Keep the door locked."

"I will."

"Don't let anyone in here unless—"

"Unless they have a warrant. Got it."

He shook his head at my curt tone. "I'm just trying to do my job here, Grace."

I sat there for a few minutes after he was gone until my curiosity got the best of me again. I headed straight for the living room, for the window, wondering if any of the boys filtered back into the neighborhood. I shoved it open, jumping and yelping when I saw Cody was standing there. "Shit!"

He was leaning back against railing, his arms crossed over his chest, staring off into the distance.

His eyes shifted my direction when I cursed, his gaze scanning me in the darkness, slowly taking me in from head to toe. "Have I ever told you how bangin' you look in that uniform?"

Rolling my eyes, I climbed out onto the fire escape to join him, not bothering to respond to that. "What happened?"

"With what?"

"You know what," I said. "What did my father say to you?"

"Oh. *That*." He laughed under his breath. "He just said some shit about respect and superiority and doing my family and neighborhood proud and whatever whatever... same bullshit Cormac gets off on railing into me about."

My brow furrowed. "He didn't say anything about me?"

"Not directly, but the message was there. He said I needed to *learn boundaries*..." He threw up the finger quotes with a roll of his eyes. "And to *keep my hands off of what doesn't belong to me.* Asked me if I understood was he was getting at."

"And you shook your head."

"So you were watching."

"Of course," I said. "What did he say after that?"

"That me being Cormac's kid will only help me so much... that if I'm not careful, I might regret not heeding his warnings."

"He *threatened* you?"

He shrugged. "They're just words, Gracie. They don't mean shit."

"But he means them."

"And I told him his threats didn't scare me," he replied. "Because they don't."

"But—"

Cody reached over, grabbing ahold of me before I could really argue. I gasped into his palm when his hand covered my mouth, making sure I couldn't speak, as he pulled me to him, my back against his chest. He held me tightly, one arm around my stomach, as he leaned down to whisper in my ear. "Do you see it?"

"See what?" I mumbled into his palm, the words barely intelligible.

Cody dropped his hand, wrapping his other arm around me. "Look straight up."

I looked straight up like he told me to, but I saw nothing for a moment... nothing except for the darkness... but after squinting, I realized what he meant. It was faint, barely visible in the low level fog, almost drowned out by the vibrant city lights, but it was there.

A star.

The first star I'd seen in years.

"Make a wish," Cody said. "Fuck knows when we'll see one those again."

I stared at it for a moment.

I wish I didn't have to deal with all of this. I wish I were far away from everything... from my father, from this life, from this neighborhood. I wish we were free from Hell's Kitchen finally.

That was what I wanted to say, but I couldn't.

I couldn't, because I was afraid of jinxing it.

So instead I said the first thing that came to my

mind. "I wish it would snow."

"Snow," he whispered. "That's the same thing I wished for."

Relaxing back against him, I grasped onto his forearms and stared up at the sky until the star disappeared, vanished as quickly as it appeared.

"Soon," Cody said, and I knew he knew what it was I really wanted—a means of escape. "It'll happen soon, Gracie. I promise."

I take a bath, not because I give a crap how I look, but because I need a moment to myself. It's probably the only place in the house I'll get some privacy today. I fill up the tub with icy cold water and climb in, relaxing back, staring at the white tile wall surrounding me. I can hear Holden moving around the house and listen as he installs the air conditioner in the living room.

A sense of guilt nags at me, deep down in my chest, until my heart feels almost too heavy to beat anymore. Taking a deep breath, I hold it in my lungs as I close my eyes and slip under the water. I can hear it as the water sloshes it out, hitting the floor, the sound magnified to my clogged ears, like ocean waves crashing around me. Slowly, I open my eyes beneath the water, blinking away the sting as I stare up at the hazy ceiling.

I count in my head.

Ten.

Twenty.

Thirty seconds.

My chest already feels like it wants to explode. The pressure is too much to contain but I press on, continuing my methodic counting. I wonder if this is what it's like to suffocate... to *really* suffocate.

I wonder what would happen if I never resurfaced, if I just parted my lips and let the water rush in, flooding my lungs as I float away to nothing.

I wonder if it would hurt.

By the time I reach forty, I'm done. *So done.* My chest can't take it and my heart... my heart hurts.

It's a scary sensation, one I don't dwell in, because a loud banging on the bathroom door jars me right out of it. The air leaves my lungs in a startled whoosh, a frenzy stream of bubbles surrounding me as I resurface.

Inhaling sharply, I wipe the water from my face as I try to shake it off. The knocking continues, quieter once my ears unclog, as Holden's voice calls out. "Gracie? You okay in there?"

"Fine," I lie.

Is it a lie?

I don't know anymore.

"You almost done in there?"

"Uh, yeah," I say, shivering despite the warm air. Jesus, what the hell's gotten in to me? "I'll be out in a minute."

I listen to his footsteps as he walks away before I reach over and pull the plug, letting the water out of the tub. I watch as it circles the drain with such force that it creates a tiny tornado, imagining myself disappearing along with it.

Who am I kidding?

I've already disappeared.

I get out of the bathtub once the water is gone, wrapping a towel around me as I dart across the hall to my bedroom. I throw on clothes, more of the same, before pulling my hair back up and heading out to face reality again. The moment I hit the living room, I hear the dull groan, feeling the blast of cool air coming from the window.

Holden is in the kitchen again. I stroll to the doorway, leaning against the doorframe, and watch as he paces around in front of the table. His service-issued Blackberry is at his ear, but he's not talking. He pulls the phone away after a moment to press a few buttons before bringing it back up, waiting for something or someone.

I don't know.

I take a seat at the table and glance at the manual for the air conditioner as it lays open in front of me, flipped to the page on how to operate it. *Like I couldn't figure that out on my own.* I pick up a pen Holden had been using and start doodling in the margins out of boredom.

"Yeah, is the line secure?" Holden asks after a moment to whoever's on the phone. "Ten minutes? Yeah, that's great… transfer me."

I cast him a curious look. I've heard him request secured lines before, usually when he's calling somewhere where he thinks people might be listening, going around his ass to get to his elbow to ensure the phone line is untraceable.

"We're connected? Great... go ahead and put him on." He pauses for a beat. "Just one moment. She's sitting right here."

I glance up with surprise just as Holden turns to me, holding out his phone. I stare at it for a second, not moving, until he pushes it toward my face, silently telling me to take it. My heart stalls for a beat before kick starting in my chest, thumping wildly.

"Ten minutes," Holden says quietly. "Watch what you say."

The phone feels heavy when I bring it to my ear, like it can't possibly sustain the weight of whatever this phone call brings. My hands tremble, the pen shaking as I absently scribble, willing my goddamn heart to quit banging in my ears and clogging my throat. I'm so nervous because of the *what-ifs* that it takes me damn near a full minute to get my voice to even work. My brain tells me this is just some routine gotta-talk-to-a-shrink-since-I'm-worried-about-you call, but my heart... my heart is frantic because of his words.

Watch what you say...

It's somebody who can't find me.

Somebody who isn't supposed to know where I am.

Put him on...

"Hello?" I say quietly, silently cursing the sound of that meek voice. I wait, the second of silence that follows absolute torture, before I'm put out of my misery by the wrong voice greeting me.

Disappointment is a son of a bitch.

My father walked me home from school every day.

Every. Fucking. Day.

Every afternoon when I stepped out those doors, he stood there, in the same spot, waiting for me. He probably thought it would thwart me from seeing Cody, but the fact was he couldn't watch over me every hour of every day.

Thank God.

I breathed a sigh of relief one Friday after dismissal when I didn't find him standing there. He said he wouldn't be. He said he was going out of town with Cormac. Usually I hated being left alone during his trips, but after his recent bout of hovering, I was grateful for a reprieve.

It was cold, so cold I could see my cloud of breath. Even bundled up and wearing thick black tights, I was still shivering. I walked fast, trying to make it home quickly, but my footsteps stalled when I neared my apartment building.

Cody was there.

He was wearing jeans and his black hoodie, his hands in the pockets and the hood up over his head. A brown paper grocery bag sat at his feet as he leaned against the old brick by the entrance.

I smiled as I approached him, calling out his name, but my expression fell when he looked over at me. His eyes were bloodshot, part of his face swelling, a deep reddish hue covering the left side of his face, the darkest of it along his cheekbone.

"Cody? Are you okay?"

Rushing forward, I reached for him, cupping his cheek and lightly stroking the bruised skin. He grabbed my wrist, pulling my hand away, as a smile touched his lips. It was sullen, not the happy smile that made my knees weak. "I'm good, Gracie."

"You don't *look* good."

"But I am." Pulling my hand up, he lightly kissed the back of it. "I'm always good when I'm with you."

I stared at him, studying his face. The bruise was fresh, the edges of it still framed with pink, not even old enough to turn purple yet, but it would. It was going to be a doozy.

"What happened?" I asked. "Did you get in another fight or something?"

"You could say that," he said. "Not a big deal, though. Looks worse than it is. Asshole just sucker punched me."

"Who did?"

"Doesn't matter." He sighed, dropping my hand to pick up the grocery bag. "I heard from a reliable source that the old man was out of town, though, so I was hoping we could hang out for a bit. I could use the company."

Before I could even ask what was in the bag, he tilted it so I could see inside, bottles clanking as he did. A six-pack of Guinness. I wasn't sure if this was a celebration or a pity part, but I wasn't going to deny him either way. Cody was usually the one comforting me. Anytime he needed it in return, I would be his.

"Do you want to come up to the apartment?"

"Sure." There was no hesitation this time. He

didn't need ten seconds to think about it. "Do you want me to take the fire escape?"

"No need," I said. "You can use the stairs."

For the first time ever, I let someone through the front door of the apartment, someone who didn't have a warrant to enter. Before I might have been skirting rules and twisting words, but this was blatant disregarding, and I didn't feel a stitch of regret about it. Cody walked over and plopped down on the couch, setting the bag on the floor by his feet. Without hesitation, he pulled out a beer. "You wouldn't happen to have a bottle opener around here, would you?"

"Of course," I said, heading into the kitchen to grab the bottle opener from the drawer. I brought it out to him, watching as he popped the top. "Do you want me to put the rest of them in the fridge?"

"Nah, don't bother." He grabbed my arm and yanked me onto the couch beside him. I laughed, relaxing as he put one arm around me before taking a long pull from the bottle, grimacing. "It tastes like shit, whether it's warm or cold. This way we won't have to keep getting up."

"If it's disgusting, why do you drink it?"

"Why do you drink coffee?"

"Because I like it."

"Well, I like Guinness," he said. "I drink it for the feeling, not the flavor."

I snuggled up against him as he drank. He offered me a sip and I took it, confirming what he said: *disgusting*. I wanted to ask him more about what happened, who he got into a fight with, what happened to his face, but I didn't want to push him for answers.

"You know, when we were kids, I used to think you were just fucking with me when you said you didn't watch television," he said after a moment as silence enveloped the room. "I mean, who the hell doesn't watch TV, you know? It still blows my mind."

My father didn't own televisions.

He wouldn't have them in his house.

He said reality was twisted enough... he didn't need our minds warped with fictionalized accounts of it. I'd seen movies of course, ones I'd snuck into with Cody without my father knowing, but otherwise it was off limits.

Most electronics were, frankly.

No cell phones.

No computers.

I lived in the technological Stone Age.

"It's not hard to go without when you've never had," I said. "It's when you get a taste and then you're denied something that you start to crave it."

Cody smiled then, the smile I loved, before laughing lightly. "Don't I know it, baby."

He drank while we relaxed, talking about everything but nothing of importance. I knocked out my weekend homework while he helped here and there, giving me answers to my math when I stumbled over problems. Cody was smart. If he could only stay out of trouble, school would be a breeze for him.

I was finishing up a worksheet for history when Cody ripped a piece of paper out of one of my notebooks. From the corner of my eye, I saw him fold it into a small triangle before fishing around in my school bag, pulling out a pair of scissors. Smiling, I watched as he started cutting it, randomly making jagged edges and patterns along the sides of it. He unfolded it when he finished, opening it up to reveal an elaborate snowflake.

He made them all the time when we were kids. He'd write along the edges and slip them to me, little presents of love whenever he could tell I was feeling sad. It had been years since he'd made one, though. That was before he began to sneak out at night, back before he learned the art of scaling fire escapes and tapping on windows.

I used to try to return the gesture, try to make him one, but mine were always an utter mess. I accidentally cut them in half most of the time.

Reaching over, Cody grabbed a pen from my bag. I wondered what he was writing, what sort of secret he was spilling along the edges of the paper.

When he was finished, he handed it to me. I took it carefully, regarding him for a moment before glancing down at the snowflake, reading his writing.

I really want to touch your boob.

Laughter burst from me. I shoved him playfully, and he wrapped his arms around me, knocking my homework onto the floor. The sky outside was starting to darken while in the living room his hands started to roam. He groped and touched me through my clothes, getting exactly what he wanted, before his hand ran beneath the fabric of my skirt, slipping into my underwear.

I didn't stop him.

His lips met mine, his kiss frenzied. Discarded bottles surrounded us, scattering when I accidentally kicked some trying to take off my tights. I started to fully undress but he stopped me, whispering against my mouth. "Keep the uniform on."

My cheeks burned from blush, but he didn't see. It was dark and he was too occupied with other parts of me. He rubbed and rubbed and rubbed between my thighs as he sucked on my neck, teeth nipping the skin. He was going to leave a mark, but I didn't care.

That was why they invented turtlenecks.

The pressure inside of me built and built, like nothing I'd ever felt before, until it built so much I couldn't contain it anymore. I cried out when pleasure rushed through me. Before I could even get a grip on what I was feeling, Cody unbuckled his pants and pulled me onto his lap.

Panic seized me for a split second as I slid down on him. It was uncomfortable again, not as much as last time, but I still wasn't used to the feeling of him being inside of me. I didn't know what I was doing, so I just moved my hips, hoping he was getting something out of it. His lips parted and he let out a soft sigh as he closed his eyes, leaning his head back on the couch.

"Just like that, Gracie," he whispered. "Fucking perfect."

It didn't take long again until he grunted, gripping my hips tightly and thrusting up a few times, finishing. Afterward, we lay on the couch, me in his arms, as that word echoed through my head.

70

Perfect.

Fucking *perfect*.

Except... it wasn't.

Perfect would have been us not having to sneak around. Perfect would have been him without a black eye. Perfect would have been my wish coming true.

"Did you get suspended again?" I asked curiously after a while. We were both dressed, for the most part. "Did they kick you out for fighting?"

"No, this didn't happen at school."

"Oh, so school is still going okay?"

"I wouldn't know," he said. "I haven't been."

I pulled back to look at him. "What do you mean?"

"I mean I stopped going."

I gaped at him. "But you're so close to graduating. How are you going to find another school to take you now?"

"I'm not," he said. "There's no point. A degree isn't going to do shit for me in these streets, Gracie."

"But you didn't want—"

"I know," he said, cutting me off. I didn't have to finish because he knew what I was thinking. "But sometimes we have to make choices we fucking hate to get what we want out of life. A little compromise never hurt anybody."

As he said that, all I could do was stare at his battered face. Whatever this compromise was, it certainly hurt him. I was trying to wrap my head around it, trying to makes sense of what he was saying. I was trying to think of the words to explain what I was feeling, but I never got a chance.

71

Because my dreams?

They went right up in flames.

It started when I heard a key in the door, the lock turning, the clicking echoing through the living room.

Cody heard it, too.

He was on his feet instantly.

Panicked, I jumped up, trying to clean up the empty beer bottles but there wasn't enough time.

"Get out of here," I hissed, pushing Cody toward the window. He shoved it open, and I cringed at the loud groan of old wood. The sound was deafening. He was slipping out, the metal banging when he scaled the fire escape, just as the last lock clicked and the door shoved open.

My father appeared.

He looked right at me as I stood in front of the open window, visibly trembling, with an empty beer bottle in my hand that I was trying to conceal. It only took him a second to put the pieces together as his eyes swept along the living room.

Before I knew it, he was running, disappearing back out the door. *Shit.* I hoped Cody made it, that he was gone before he could get caught, and climbed out onto the fire escape to try to warn him before it was too late.

My breath caught as I look down. *Busted.*

Cormac Moran stood on the sidewalk near his town car. Cody was beside his father, shivering his ass off in the cold evening air. He wasn't wearing his hoodie. My gaze darted behind me, toward the couch in the apartment. His hoodie was still on the floor along with some other discarded clothes.

Oh God.

Oh no.

My knees went weak.

I had to grip onto the railing.

I watched down below as my father burst outside, his voice booming like thunder as he lunged right for Cody. "You little son of a bitch! You think you can come into my house? You think you can violate my daughter? You think you can do that and *get away with it*?"

Cormac intervened before my father could throw any punches, stepping between the two of them. I couldn't hear what the man said, but whatever it was silenced my father... at least temporarily. The men talked heatedly for a minute before my father turned away from them and stormed back inside. I watched, frozen, as Cormac roughly grabbed Cody by his shirt, throwing him against the passenger side of the town car, so hard it left a dent. Cody raised his hands in a sign of surrender as Cormac verbally laid into him. After shoving him back against it again, Cormac finally let go to walk around to the driver's side.

Cody paused briefly, glancing up at me on the fire escape, before getting in the car.

They hadn't even yet pulled away from the curb when my father returned to the apartment. I heard the front door close and heard his footsteps along the wooden floor. I braced myself for his rage. I was prepared for disgust, even ready to feel the man's hatred.

What I got was far, far worse.

"I'm disappointed in you, Grace Callaghan," he

said, his voice laced with dejection. "I thought you were better than this."

"Grace." My father's voice is always gruff, like he's constantly fighting to keep his emotions in check, but I know that's just his natural tone. "It's great to hear your voice again."

Closing my eyes, I swallow thickly. "Dad."

I love my father.

I do.

But he made this bed that I'm forced to lie in, day in and day out, all alone in this ironic little town, so it's hard not to feel some resentment. He gave me life, sure, but I also blame him for taking my life away. I always knew he did bad things, always knew he hung around bad people, but I never knew the scope of it until the day Holden let me read the thirty-page indictment against him.

My father was linked to a body count higher than Ted Bundy's.

It's hard to reconcile that fact with the man who raised me.

My father was Dr. Jekyll.

The man on the phone is the evil Mr. Hyde.

Connor Callaghan.

He got to keep his last name.

"How are you?" he asks. "You staying safe? How's school?"

He fires questions at me, innocently enough, but I

74

have to think through every answer before saying anything at all. Something as simple as conversation about the weather could lead the wrong person right to my front door.

I say I'm fine, people are nice, school's great, but the truth is I stopped going months ago and I haven't made a single friend in this place. Holden leans against the counter and listens in on the conversation, knowing I'm lying my ass off.

Maybe I'm better at being dishonest than I think.

I absently scribble in the margins of the manual as my father babbles on and on, doing what I always do—signing my name.

My *fake* name.

Over and over, practicing until it practically bleeds from my fingertips.

Ten minutes isn't that long, not when you haven't spoken to someone in over a year, but there's a lot of awkward silence when you have nothing to say. I'm ashamed by the relief I feel when Holden pushes away from the counter, tapping two fingers against the face of his watch, telling me time is up.

"I have to go," I say, interrupting my father as he's talking about something. I don't know. I stopped paying attention.

He lets out a deep sigh. "Just a few more years, Grace, and I'll be out of this mess. A few more years and we can start over as a family."

I don't respond to that.

I've faced reality.

There's no starting over for him and I.

"Goodbye, Dad."

I pull the phone away from my ear and hit the button to end the call before holding it out to Holden. I drop the pen after he takes the phone, leaning back in the chair and running my hands down my face. "Please don't ever do that to me again."

Holden pulls out the chair across from me and sits. He's quiet for a moment, and I glance over, meeting his eyes, seeing the frown on his lips. He thought he was doing me a favor, that talking to someone I knew in that other world would pacify me, but hearing my father's voice again only made these feelings worse.

I haven't seen the man in a year, yet he's still controlling my life.

I've never felt so smothered.

"You wanted it to be somebody else on the phone, didn't you?"

I scoff. "What makes you say that?"

Holden motions toward the manual I'd been doodling in. One glance at it gives me my answer. I'd absently scribbled Cody's name more than once without thinking. Picking up the pen again, I quickly scratch out every instance of it, knowing there's a rule against leaving shit like that around. There are ways, of course, of communicating with the past... these untraceable phone calls, letters hand delivered by Marshals that are burned after reading.

But in my case, it wasn't possible.

I look around the kitchen, looking at everything except for Holden. We've had this conversation about Cody before, and I'm not in the mood to have it again. "Can I ask you something, inspector?"

From the corner of my eye, I see him grimace. He hates being called that about as much as he hates being deemed a handler.

'Just call me Holden,' he'd insisted. *'Not Inspector, not Marshal... just Holden.'*

Holden is his last name, technically. I didn't even know that until I spotted it on some paperwork a few months back. *United States Marshals Service Inspector Brian Holden.*

I've never called him Brian.

He probably doesn't even realize I know that's his name.

"You can ask me anything," he says, tearing the manual away from me and tossing it across the room, onto the kitchen counter, when I start doodling in it again. "As long as you look at me when you do."

I stare at him, still clutching the pen, and defiantly start scribbling right on the top of the kitchen table. He doesn't stop me, knowing he really can't. The Marshals Service paid for this table, but it belongs to *me*. Holden wants to intervene, though. I can see his fingers twitching.

"Have you ever lost a witness?"

It's kind of funny, I think, that I'm considered a *witness*, considering I haven't witnessed a fucking thing. Unless the injustice of humanity counts...

He hesitates. "Define 'lost'."

"As in 'died'," I say. "Has anyone ever died on your watch?"

"No."

"Never?"

"Never," he says. "No witness has ever died that

77

followed the rules."

"And the ones that didn't follow the rules? How many of them have died?"

"About thirty."

Thirty.

My father's personal body count is higher than that.

"Out of how many?"

"There are about seventeen thousand people under protection."

That momentarily leaves me speechless.

That's a lot of people living lives that don't belong to them. I wonder how many feel like me. I wonder how many leave because of it, how many risk death, risk becoming one of those unlucky thirty, just for the chance to be themselves again.

"I know thirty doesn't seem like a lot," Holden continues. "But it's thirty lives we tried to save... lives we *would've* saved, if they had just followed the rules. It's a senseless death, and I pray to God there's never a thirty-one."

I nod, tinkering with the pen, scratching marks into the table until Holden reaches his breaking point. He covers my hand with his own, prying the pen from my grip.

"The program works, Gracie," he says, pocketing the pen before I can take it back. "You just have to learn to work with it."

Standing, Holden starts gathering his things, and I watch as he pulls himself together to leave. The tie goes on, his badged slipped around his neck, before he puts on his holster to conceal his gun beneath his coat.

I know he's still standing in front of me, but I suddenly feel utterly alone.

"I have some other business to attend to, so it'll be a while before I make another scheduled visit," he says. "It'll probably be closer to Christmas."

Christmas.

It's only three weeks, but it feels so far away.

He's never stayed gone so long before.

"Call me if you need me," he says, pulling out an envelope and dropping it on the table. "Here's your stipend for the month."

I grab the envelope, pulling it into my lap, and skim through the cash as he finishes getting ready. There's fifteen hundred dollars in it. My father used to leave me that much when he left for a weekend.

Holden strolls around the table to where I'm sitting on his way to the door, placing his hand on my shoulder and squeezing. "Happy Birthday, Gracie. Here's to many more…"

The sound of tapping glass was so faint I felt like it had to be a figment of my imagination, a phantom echo from somewhere deep down in my soul. My head turned, slowly, the sense of disappointment already brewing in my gut, preparing for the let down.

It had been two weeks.

Two weeks since Cody scurried out that window

only to get caught on the way down. He hadn't been hanging around the neighborhood with his friends. He didn't show up at the diner while I was having breakfast. He certainly hadn't come *here*.

I expected to see nothing, but my eyes caught a sliver of green in the moonlight. He was there, crouched on the fire escape, peering in the window at me. His face was cast in shadows from the darkness, but I could make out bruising on his face, the marks moving down his jawline, toward a freshly busted lip that lined up almost perfectly with the scar that runs down his chin.

A scar his father caused the first time he hurt him, back when we were just little kids. 'He's going to be a man someday,' Cormac used to say. 'Might as well start treating him like one.' By treating, he'd meant beating. And by a man, he meant one of his guys that run the streets. Cody was never a *son* to him. Cody was just flesh and blood… the pieces that make up a person. Cormac never cared what else existed inside of the boy.

He never cared Cody wanted more than his neighborhood.

But looking at Cody at that moment, I knew the neighborhood had finally gotten its claws into him. There wouldn't be any secret smiles from him this time. No more whispered promises of 'soon'.

Standing up, I gave a look around the quiet apartment out of pure instinct before walking over to the window and shoving it open, not caring about the noise it made. There was nobody there with me. I pushed it open as far as it would go, a blast of cold air

80

hitting me right away. Two weeks were all it took for the warmth to move out and the cold to seep in, like his absence made more than just *me* mourn. The temperature finally dipped below freezing, the air damp and sky covered in clouds. I can tell the metal railing is slick, the steps icy.

I shivered, wrapping my arms around myself right away. I was wearing his hoodie. He never came back for it. I started to climb out to join him but his hands grasped my arms, stopping me before I could come through the window.

"It's too cold," he said. "Don't come out here. You'll freeze."

"Do you…?" I paused. "Do you want to come in?"

He didn't answer that question.

He didn't have to.

His ten second hesitation returned, turning to twenty… thirty… forty…

A minute later, after nothing from him, I knelt down on the floor, knowing he wasn't going to move. He stared at me like he was looking through me, studying me, looking for answers to an equation he was desperate to solve.

"I'm glad you're here," I told him.

"I shouldn't be," he said. "I was told to stay away from you."

"My father—"

"Not yours," he cut in before I could even get it out. "Your father didn't do it. He has no say over me."

"Yours," I whispered, reaching through the window for him. He didn't stop me as my hand covered the massive bruise on his face. "He did this to you."

81

Cody pulled his eyes away from me then, like I was just too painful to face. "Cormac figured since I wasn't listening, pounding it into me was the only way to get his point across."

"I just… I don't understand it," I said, fingertips trailing his jawline before tracing his lips, reaching the scar. "You're his family."

"Family doesn't mean shit to him," Cody said. "Family is just the people they go after when they want to send you a message. That's it. They're either a liability or an advantage, depending on which side of the game you're playing. And Cormac? He doesn't believe in hauling around dead weight. You know that."

There was no bitterness to his voice. He spoke matter-of-factly, like this was normal for families, like fathers were supposed to treat their children this way. But I didn't accept it and I never would. It wasn't our fault they did the things they did. We shouldn't have been the ones who faced punishment. "It's not right."

"But it's life," he said. "It's my life."

"You don't want it to be."

"But it is," he said quietly. "It is."

I wasn't sure what to say.

I knew there was no room for argument, knew that any pleading or pestering from my lips would fall on deaf ears. We had been around in circles, back and forth, flipped upside down, and we ultimately ended up here after everything.

"It is what it is," he continued, realizing I was conceding, that I wasn't going to try to argue with him. I could almost see the relief on his face, but in his eyes there was something else... something I had never seen from him before: *surrender*. His eyes had always been full of spark, but there was nothing there now. There was no more fight left for his own life. "And like I said, I shouldn't be here, but I really needed to give you your present."

I frowned. "My birthday isn't until tomorrow."

Seventeen.

No longer sixteen, but it still wasn't eighteen.

Not yet.

"Close enough," he said, reaching into his pants pocket and grabbing something, pulling it out and concealing it in his fist. "I didn't have a chance to wrap it, and well... fuck it. I've never been good at that shit."

He held his hand out toward me as he opened it. There, in his palm, lay a silver necklace. A smile crept up on my lips when I reached for it, taking it from him. A locket. Perfectly round, a tad bigger than a quarter. On the front was a snowflake, the edges of it framed in diamonds. I would've asked if they were real, but I knew Cody. He'd never buy me something fake. Flipping it over, I ran my thumb over the back, feeling the grooves from the words engraved in it.

Gracie—

Soon.

—C

"It's beautiful," I whispered.

He nudged my hand. "Open it."

I flicked the locket open, my eyes meeting an old picture. It was Cody and I, back when we were just little kids, before we ever fell in love and realized

83

what a harsh world we lived in. I was grinning at the camera, happy as could be, while Cody just stared at me.

"Couldn't keep my eyes off you back then," he said. "Guess I loved you even when I was ten."

I traced the outline of our young faces before closing the locket again, clutching it tightly in my palm. Emotions swirled through me, heavy and tumultuous, like a brewing storm. I felt the tears building in my eyes, felt the lump in my throat. It was the greatest gift anyone had ever given me before.

I met his eyes, smiling. "Thank you."

He nodded as if to say 'you're welcome', but he didn't say the words. Instead, he looked away from me, tilting his head up toward the sky. It was drizzling a bit, had been all day, the light rain hitting his long lashes. He blinked it away as he lowered his head again, once more meeting my gaze.

His expression of relief faded away. Reaching through the window, he cupped my chin with his cold hand, tilting my face toward him. Carefully, he leaned forward, kissing my mouth. It was barely a peck, but I was shaking, shivering, breathing in his warmth when he whispered against my lips, "I won't see you for a while after this, Gracie."

The coldness from his hand, the chilling tone of is voice, seeped through my skin, freezing my insides when I absorbed those words. I opened my eyes. "What?"

"It's for the best," he said, "that we don't see each other for a while."

He pulled back, dropping his hand. I gaped at

84

him, my mind trying to process those words, but my heart beat too loudly for it to understand.

"For the best?" I asked. "I don't understand. How can it be for the best that we don't see each other?"

"Because it is," he said, as if those words made any sense, as if they offered anything in the way of an explanation of how he could actually think him being absent from my world made anything *better*. He was my pulse. He was the air I breathed. He was the sun that shined on this shit show of a life I'd been given.

"That's stupid. That's just... that's the stupidest thing I've ever heard. Because it is? *Because it is?* There's nothing *for the best* about this, Cody. I don't want to be without you. I *love* you."

"I know."

"You know? So why? Why would you say it's for the best?"

"Because it is," he said again, running his hands through his damp hair, making the locks stick straight up. He eyed me, his expression earnest, as if he was trying to get me to understand something with just a look.

But I couldn't.

I didn't understand.

He let out a deep sigh of exasperation that broke something inside of me, thawing the ice that gripped me so I could no longer stop the flood. Tears broke free from my eyes, streaming down my cheeks, as my breath caught in my throat.

This couldn't be happening.

"You're leaving me," I gasped, trying to make my voice sound calm like his is, but my panic was too much. "On my birthday?"

"Tomorrow's your birthday," he whispered.

His response hit me like a ton of bricks, snapping something. I didn't think. I reacted. My chest was heavy and my heart hurt, the pain seizing my muscles and controlling them. My hands thrust out, and I shoved him, hard, knocking him backward on the fire escape. He slips on the slick metal, dropping right on his ass, the fire escape rattling loudly.

He got traction again and climbed to his feet. Part of me wished this were just some sick, sick prank, the worst joke ever told. I wanted him to climb through the window and pull me into his arms and tell me he wouldn't dream of ever leaving me alone. But ten seconds passed… I counted them in my head… and he didn't make a move.

He didn't say anything.

My shoulders slumped. My heart was broken and he just stood there, so whole, his hands slipping into his pocket like he was waiting for something.

If he were waiting for me to tell him this was okay, it wasn't going to happen.

Because it wasn't okay.

It *wasn't*.

"I love you, Gracie," he said quietly. "I love you with everything in me. I always will, you know."

I closed my eyes. "Yet you're walking away. You're leaving me. You're just going to go down that fire escape and what… disappear from my life?"

"Impossible," he said. "Just because you won't see me doesn't mean I'm gone."

"That's easy for you to say."

"Yeah, it is. It's easy to say, because it's true. You can break people apart, but you can't rob them of what's *them*. You'll never be without me, because I'll always be part of you, just like you're in me, Gracie. You're my soul, love."

My tears started falling harder.

He gave it ten seconds then.

Ten seconds before he turned around and walked away.

I collapsed as it all purged from me, my body viciously shaking as every part of me hurt. The cold filtered into the apartment from the open window, the heater no match for the icy air. It infused into everything around me, freezing my world as I fell to pieces on the floor.

"Gracie!"

Cody's voice held a hint of emotion as he shouted my name from the street somewhere. I forced myself to my feet, my vision blurred from my tears, and climbed out onto the icy fire escape. The moment I stepped out, I felt the coldness hit my face, wetness that had nothing to do with crying.

My first thought was maybe he changed his mind, maybe he saw how wrong this was, but no... I knew that couldn't be so. He wouldn't have done this, wouldn't have said those words, if he weren't sure. I blinked away more tears as I glanced down, seeing Cody standing along the curb staring up at me. White specks fell down around him from the sky, sporadic snowflakes, just enough to make out in the darkness.

"Look, Gracie," he called out. "Your wish came true."

No, I thought, as he walked away.

It hadn't come true at all.

Hours pass after Holden leaves.

Hours that mean nothing.

Hours that don't matter to me.

Because eighteen looks exactly like seventeen, and it certainly doesn't *feel* any different. I don't feel older or wiser or any more mature. It's not magic, like Cinderella's carriage transforming at midnight because of some spell.

The only difference is I'm not a minor anymore.

My decisions are my own now. Nobody can stop me from making my own choices. They don't have to like them, but I'm the one who had to live with whatever happens.

Me, not them.

So I give myself those hours.

Before I find myself walking out the front door.

I'm not sure what possesses me to do it, what lights the fire under my ass that makes me put on real clothes and actually fix my hair. I don't know what possesses me to leave the house, to get in that piece of shit car and start to drive. I don't know what possesses me to speed right by that Snowflake city limit sign again.

I don't know, but I do it.

And this time, I keep going.

I packed one bag before I left the house.

Just one.

That's it.

It's easy to condense this life into one bag, because there hasn't really been much to it.

I drive to Phoenix.

It's a three-hour trip. It's dark, and the Chevy is spewing smoke again by the time I get there, the repairs just a Band-Aid on a gaping wound. It barely holds on until I reach my destination.

The airport.

Using some of the money Holden left, I buy a ticket on the first flight out of Arizona. Maybe it's irrational, and maybe it's stupid, making this decision on a whim, but I'm tired of thinking. I'm tired of suffocating. I'm tired of being alone.

This isn't my life.

And I'm not going to live it anymore.

I wore Cody's hoodie to class.

Sister Abigail singled me out for breaking the dress code the moment I stepped into Calculus, ignoring the fifteen other girls in class with too short skirts and a hell of a lot of unapproved hair 'dos. I ignored her, refusing to take it off, for the first time in my life talking back to a nun. She sent me straight to the principal's office for reprimanding, but I didn't care.

I was tired of caring when nobody else seems to anymore.

"You know the rules," the principal said as I sat across from him in the lavish office on the fancy leather chair that my father helped pay for with the outrageous tuition at this place. "You're only allowed to wear certain approved garments."

"So approve this one," I said, "then I'll be allowed to wear it."

"It doesn't work that way."

"Why not?"

He sighed exasperatedly. "Because it doesn't. So take it off and—"

"No."

He raised his eyebrows at my denial. "No?"

"No," I said again. "Why do I have to follow the dress code when none of the other girls in this place do?"

He didn't answer that, but I knew the answer. None of them were Conner Callaghan's daughter. I knew my father well enough to know he called and complained, voicing his expectations for my schooling. He wanted the dress code followed, so they'd enforce it... on *his* little girl, at least.

"What's gotten into you?" the principal asked in lieu of answering my question. "This isn't like you at all, Grace."

I wanted to tell him he didn't know that... he *couldn't* know that... because he didn't know me at all. The only person who really ever knew me turned his back on me, leaving me with nothing but a heavy silver locket around my neck and a ratty old hoodie he didn't bother to take back, and nobody was going to take them from me.

Especially not today.

Not on my birthday.

He stared at me for a moment before shaking his head at my lack of response, knowing conversation about this was pointless. He said he had stuff to do and he supposed I'd be keeping him company, since I couldn't go back to class until I conformed to the dress code.

I slouched down in the chair instead of complying, getting comfortable, and sat there until final dismissal.

As soon as the bell rang, I stood up and turned to walk out, hearing him clear his throat behind me. "Wait a moment, Miss Callaghan."

I ignored him as I strolled outside, my brow furrowing when I found the hallways empty, all of the other students still in their classrooms, even though the day was over. The principal came out of his office after me, urging me to stop, but I refused to listen.

He could suspend me for all I cared.

The overnight snow hadn't stuck, but the sidewalks were still slick with ice, meaning the walk home was really going to suck.

Especially with who would insist on accompanying me.

As soon as I stepped out onto the stone steps, I saw my father standing in his usual spot, waiting. I considered walking right past him, considered pretending he wasn't even there, when something caught my eye in the distance. Flashing lights in my peripheral startled me, stalling my footsteps.

It happened quickly.

Out of nowhere, cars screeched to a halt right in front of the school, red and blue lights filling the overcast sky. Chaos erupted, men rushing onto the sidewalk, some with uniforms and guns, others wearing suits with shiny badges. My heart raced as adrenaline coursed through my body. I felt like I was going to faint as dizziness took over.

My father was thrown to the sidewalk before he could utter a single word.

"Connor Callaghan, you're under arrest."

I wasn't sure who said it. There were too many of them. My father's hands were forced behind his back as handcuffs were secured on his thick wrists.

What the hell is happening?

"Dad?" I cried, stunned to see blood streaking his face from a scrape on his cheek. They were being rough with him. "Oh God… what's going on?"

His eyes instantly sought me out. He looked calm, relaxed, not a worry in the world, like he wasn't even surprised he was being arrested.

"It's just a mistake, Grace," he said, ignoring the officers as they read him his rights. "That's all this is… a big mistake. I'll take care of it. Don't worry. I'll be back home before you know it."

He didn't have a chance to say anything more. In a blink, he was being hauled away, shoved into the back of an idling police cruiser.

I was still trying to wrap my head around what was happening when a woman approached. "Grace Callaghan?"

My eyes flickered to her.

She introduced herself. I didn't even catch her name. I was too busy watching my father disappear down the street. My mind was a flurry of frantic thoughts when the woman's voice again cut through the haze. "Grace, I'm going to need you to come with me."

I looked at her then. *Really* looked at her. She was young, maybe mid-twenties, wearing a run of the mill NYPD uniform. "Excuse me?"

"I need to take you down to the station. Don't worry—you're not in trouble."

Don't worry.

That was the same thing my father said.

I didn't listen.

I was *worried*.

"Why? What did I do?"

"Nothing," she said. "You did nothing wrong. This isn't your fault."

She used *that* tone on me... the tone that's reserved for children and the mentally unstable. I wondered, looking at me, which one of those she saw. "Then why do I need to go?"

"Your father's going away for a while. Since you're still a minor, we'll need to temporarily place you."

"Place me in *what*? A cell? Are you going to lock me up, too?"

"Of course not," she said. "Social services will place you in the care of an adult."

"This is all a mistake." I shook my head and took a step back. This woman seriously lost her damn mind. "You heard him. It's a *mistake*. It has to be. He's going to take care of it. You'll see."

The woman smiled sadly. It felt like she was mocking me. *Poor little girl doesn't know what she's saying.* "I'm afraid it's not a mistake. Your father is in serious trouble. He's not coming home anytime soon."

"Regardless," I said, taking another step back. And another. And another. "I'm not a little kid. I can take care of myself. I don't need to be *placed* anywhere."

I turned around just as she reached for me, catching my arm. Panic seized me, and I reacted instinctively, yanking my arm back away. Without another thought, I broke into a sprint, darting away from the woman and rushing back into the school building.

I wasn't at all surprised when she followed, shouting.

I darted through the halls and right out the back door, ducking through alleys and shoving past people when they got in my way. The sidewalk was practically a slip and slide, nearly knocking me on my ass when I rounded corners. My breath was coming out in sharp gasps and my body was trembling, but I didn't know if it was from fear or from the cold.

I lost the woman somewhere behind the school, but that did nothing to ease my worry, because as soon as I turned onto the block for my apartment building, I saw the cars. The same ones from the school, maybe, or they might have been others. I didn't know. All I knew was the place was crawling with police.

I couldn't go home.

I couldn't go home, but I didn't know where else to go.

Dropping my head down, I swiftly turned the other direction, going the only other place I could go for help.

The Morans.

I ducked inside their building when someone opened the front door, ignoring the shouts of protest from the doorman as I ran right past the elevator, dodging for the stairs. I was wheezing by the time I made it to the tenth floor, doubling over to try to catch my breath as I banged on the apartment door.

It was opened within moments, and I glanced up, meeting Cormac Moran's gaze. His brow furrowed when he saw me, and edge of something in his eyes. *Anger*.

My father may have never liked Cody, but it was nothing compared to how Cormac felt about me. I overheard him once say I was nothing more than an unfortunate inconvenience that got in the way of my father ever being somebody someday.

"I need to see Cody," I said... or tried to say, anyway. The words were rushed, jumbled, barely intelligible to my own ears, but he seemed to understand.

"He's not here," Cormac said.

"Where is he?" I asked, standing up straight, wishing my hands would stop shaking and my lungs would cooperate. "How can I find him?"

"I don't know."

"You don't know?"

"No, I don't."

"But…" How could he not know? "I need to see him."

"I don't know where he is," Cormac said again, stressing the words, the anger now tingeing his voice. "He left here last night and hasn't returned."

"I know… I saw him last night, but he left and… he left, but I need to see him, and I thought…"

"You thought he'd be home," he said, "but he isn't, so you should go."

He started to shut the door, but I reached out, slamming my hand against it, stopping him. That anger in his eyes flared, but I was too frazzled to care. I knew the man has one hell of a temper, had seen proof of it on Cody's face way too many times, but I didn't think he'd ever hit me.

At least I *hoped*.

"Look, I'm sorry, but I don't know where else to go. My father was arrested, and there are police everywhere and—"

"Connor was arrested? For what?"

"I don't know. He said it was all just a mistake."

"I'm sure he's right." Cormac leaned against the doorframe as he crossed his arms over his chest. He studied me like he was trying to decide whether or not I was lying, like he thought maybe this was all some game. After a moment, he shook his head. "Go home. Wait it out. It'll blow over."

I tried to argue, to tell him I couldn't go there, when the door slammed in my face.

It was hard to know where to turn to when you didn't have anybody anymore. I kept my head down as I strolled around Hell's Kitchen, dodging away from police cars, seeking out Cody. I wasn't sure where to find him. I'd never had to do it before. He always just knew when I needed him. He always knew to come to me.

It was well after dark, and I was cold and shivering, my feet hurting and head pounding. I made my way back to the school, back to where this day all went to hell, and sat down on the steps in front of the building.

The neighborhood was quiet. I sat there for a while before the doors behind me opened. My heart stalled for a beat as I swung around, but it wasn't anybody I expected to see. My principal stood there, huddled up in a thick coat, his hand still on the door. He eyed me curiously, frowning.

It wasn't a church, but it was the closest I'd ever come to belonging to one. The man couldn't offer me sanctuary here. He had no obligation to help me, but part of me hoped he would. Standing up, I wrapped my arms around myself. "Please don't turn me in. I'll leave. I will. I just… I don't have anywhere to go."

His frown deepened as he motioned toward the building. "Come in out of the cold, Grace. You'll be safe here."

Safe. I wasn't sure I trust that word. Safe was something only Cody ever made me feel, and he was gone now. Where did he go?

Most of my life was spent in a box—a proverbial box,

with four familiar walls and an enclosed top, shielding me from everything outside of it. The box felt too big to break out of but too small to spend the rest of my life in, like I was locked inside a cage with no bars, the worst kind of prison there is.

Because if you can't *see* your restraints, how are you supposed to escape them?

I lived in this box until the day it collapsed, the pressure on it too great to sustain the weight of reality. And now that I'm free of my invisible chains, I don't know where to go except for where I've always been.

Hell's Kitchen.

The place looks the same at first glance, but everything feels different. *Everything.* The street is too quiet while the air is bitter cold. It's after nightfall, darkness cloaking everything, so thick even the streetlights seem to struggle cutting through it. It's the city that never sleeps, but nobody seems to be awake, like a spell was cast over the neighborhood in the wake of what happened. Cars drive through on their way to somewhere else, lights on in some of the apartments, but it's nothing like it used to be. There are no boys hanging out on the corner. There's no shouting or laughing. The fire escapes are all empty. The windows are all closed.

And the diner on the corner, once open twenty-four hours a day, 365 days a year, stands quiet, a shell of what it used to be, devastated in a fire sometime during my absence. The windows are all boarded up, the door busted. The sight of it makes my chest heavy.

I don't dwell. Not now, anyway. Instead I head to the small public library a few blocks away. It's even quieter here than it is out on the street, only a handful of people sitting around, studying. Slowly, I stroll up to the front desk, to the lone librarian on duty. She's relaxing in her chair, flipping through a magazine. "Excuse me, but do you have a computer I can use?"

She doesn't even look up. "We're closing in twenty minutes."

"It won't take me long," I say. "Just a moment, really."

She huffs, holding her hand out. "Library card."

"I, uh… well, I don't…"

Her eyes drift overtop of her magazine to meet mine. "You have to have a valid library card to use a computer."

"I do," I say. Or well, I *did*. "I just don't have it with me, but I have one. And like I said, it'll only take a moment, and it's really important. I have nowhere else to go, and I need to use a computer."

I must sound convincing, probably since it's not technically a lie, because she tosses down the magazine and shoves a clipboard toward me. "Write down your name and the time."

I offer her a smile of relief as I scribble my name down. *Grace Kennedy*.

"Upstairs," she said, taking the clipboard back. "You have twenty minutes."

I take the steps quickly, sitting down at the first empty computer I find, and open Google. I don't need twenty minutes. All I need are a few. Just a search of my father's name gives me everything Holden has

99

been keeping from me.

Connor Callaghan, murderer, is being hailed a *hero*.

I suddenly feel sick.

He's testified almost a dozen times in the past year and has been dubbed as the man to single-handedly destroy the Irish mob in Hell's Kitchen, as if he did it from the kindness of his heart and not out of selfishness. His testimony has brought down plenty of men, but Cormac Moran still walks free. The man runs the streets, released on bail for petty conspiracy charges, still awaiting judgment for his many sins.

His trial is just after Christmas.

My father again will be testifying.

Closing the browser, I shove the chair back and stand to leave. I head down the steps, eyes on my feet, and go right out the front door. The moment I step out onto the sidewalk, I nearly slam right into someone. My footsteps halt abruptly at the door, and I glance up as the person stops in front of me.

My heart races when my eyes connect with a vaguely familiar face. I don't know his name, and it takes a moment for me to place him, one of the boys who used to hang around Cody in the neighborhood. *Shit.* He looks at me, his brow furrowing as he studies my face. Confusion is laced in his features, like he thinks he might know me but he doesn't know how. And I know it's because he doesn't… he doesn't know *this* girl, the one who spent the past year in Snowflake. He's never encountered her before. We share some of the same features, sure, but I'm not entirely that girl he saw before.

My eyes dart back to the sidewalk as I quickly step around him, muttering, "Excuse me."

"Grace? Grace Callaghan?" he calls out. "Is that you?"

"You've got the wrong person," I shout back. "I'm not her."

I hurry away, glancing back only briefly to see the boy shake his head and disappear into the library.

I slept in the nurse's office, on the small cot reserved for sick students. The next morning, I was awoken by the principal and told to go to class with promises that he would handle everything for me. I didn't know what that meant, I didn't know how he could help, but I was exhausted, so exhausted... so I trusted the man.

I sat in class, in a daze, staring off into space until Sister Abigail shouted my name. My eyes sought her out in the front of the classroom as she studied me, raising her eyebrows. "You need to go to the principal's office, Grace."

Rolling my eyes, I stood up, shoving my hands in the pockets of the hoodie as I stalked toward the door. The last thing I cared about was another dress code violation lecture. I made my way to the front office, pushing the door open without knocking, sighing exasperatedly when I did. "Look, I'm not taking off the hoodie, okay?"

"Okay."

The voice that responded was not a voice I knew. I looked up, seeing a pair of bright blue eyes that I'd almost call kind if it weren't for the badge hanging around the guy's neck they were attached to. My eyes narrowed as my gaze darted straight to the principal. "This is your idea of *helping*?"

He held his hands up defensively.

The stranger chimed in. "Grace Elizabeth Callaghan?"

"Yes." I turn to him. "But I'm sure you already knew that."

The man smiled knowingly as he held out a hand for me to shake. "Grace, I'm with the U.S. Marshals Service… and you and I need to have a conversation."

The apartment is dark.

No lights shine from the windows, no shadows moving around inside. It blends in with the blackness blanketing the eerily quiet neighborhood. It's closing in on midnight and I have nowhere to go.

I've got some cash left but not a credit card. Nobody will rent me a room. I have no friends in this city, no family left, nothing except for a life I abandoned up in that apartment.

Jumping up, I grab the ladder for the fire escape, yanking it down. I struggle a bit, trying to get my footing on the metal rungs, but I carefully climb up. I try to be as quiet as possible, not wanting to disturb any of the neighbors as I scale the building, the whole way up to the fifth floor.

I pause there, crouching down on the dingy metal platform, and gaze in. It's too dark for me to make out anything inside. Hesitating, contemplating, I press my hands to the cold glass of the window, pushing up on it, trying to get the thing to budge. The window sticks, barely shifting half an inch, but it's just enough for me to slide my fingers underneath. *Unlocked.*

I struggle shoving it open, the wood groaning worse than ever before, but I manage to get it up enough to slide my body inside, out of the bitter cold.

My feet hit the wooden floor, and I close the window behind me, blocking out the cold. Turning around, I blink a few times, adjusting to the darkness, an overwhelming suffocation squeezing my chest when things come into focus.

It's empty.

Completely empty.

I shouldn't be surprised, and maybe I'm not, but it still takes me a moment to come to terms with that fact. The last time I was here, this place was packed full of belongings, *my* belongings, everything I'd been forced to leave behind. I wonder what they did with all of it. Donated it to charity? Destroyed it? Discarded it? Maybe they put it in a storage unit some place. I don't know.

All I know is it's gone.

Nothing's here.

I don't venture any further than the living room. I know it'll all look the same. The bed where I once gave myself to Cody will be missing, my bucket list of dreams covering the walls ripped away, like none of it ever happened.

Like the girl I'd been never existed.

Pressing my back against the wall, I slide down to the floor, stretching my legs out in front of me. I'm exhausted. *So exhausted*. Everything feels so different; maybe too much changed.

Maybe, just maybe, this was a mistake.

I don't know what I planned to accomplish by coming here. Like maybe I could prove Holden wrong, show him that all of this was senseless, that I don't need protected. But now that I'm here, I'm afraid to find out what's true, afraid that maybe Holden wasn't the one who was mistaken.

It's a battle between my head and my heart, and I'm too exhausted to continue the fight tonight. I'm staring across the dark room at nothing, contemplating where I go from here, wondering if I even have enough cash to make it back to Arizona, when the silence is shattered by an abrupt noise. The shrill sound stalls my heart for a beat before I reach for my bag, shifting things around inside to pull out the old cell phone. I flip it open, staring at the screen as it rings.

Blocked number.

Holden.

His service-issued Blackberry doesn't show up on Caller ID.

Before I can get my muscles to work again, before I can do anything, the ringing stops. I stare at the missed call, a sinking feeling in the pit of my stomach.

He shouldn't even know I'm gone yet. He would be preoccupied with whatever business he had to attend to and wouldn't have time to find out anything about me. But Holden isn't one to call for nothing, and I know that. If he's trying to contact me, there's a reason.

Sighing, I close the phone and set it on the floor as I stretch out, laying my head down on my bag, using it as a makeshift pillow. It's uncomfortable, but I'm too tired to care, as I snuggle up against it, pulling my arms up into the hoodie and wrapping them around myself.

Cody's hoodie.

It stopped smelling like him a long time ago, but I close my eyes and inhale anyway, trying to conjure up his scent. But all I breathe in is the dust coating the room, the stale smell from the place being vacant for so long, no air circulating. I lay there, breathing steadily, eyes squeezed shut, hoping the memories will be enough to keep me warm as I wait for morning.

I don't know when it happened, but at some point I drift off, because I'm jarred out of a deep sleep by the shrill ringing once more. My eyes open, and are immediately met with light. *Ugh.* It's morning sometime and the sun is shining just bright enough to highlight the empty room around me.

Sitting up, I cringe at the crick in my neck, my back stiff from sleeping on the hard floor. It's cold, even with the window closed, a cloud of breath surrounding me as I reach for my phone. I pick it up just as it stops ringing, knowing exactly who it's

105

going to be, and stare at the thing as it starts making noise again right away.

On the third call, back-to-back, I press the button and bring the phone to my ear. My heart beats wildly but I try to play it cool. "Hello?"

Holden, always so composed, is calm no more. "Where the hell are you? Tell me right now! I need to know!"

"I, uh... I'm at home."

"Don't lie to me, Grace, goddammit," he shouts, and the line is cracking up, but it's clear enough to detect the sheer panic in his voice. "This is serious. I know you hopped a plane. I know you're in New York. People have *seen* you in New York. This isn't the time for games!"

"I'm not lying," I say. "I'm at home."

A second of silence passes—that's it, just a second—but the silence screams louder than any of his words. Holden always knows what to say, how to handle situations, but I've rendered him momentarily speechless.

Even for a second, I know it's too much.

I'm on my feet in an instant, swaying from a bout of dizziness, my heart beating way too fast as his voice finally kicks in. "Get out of there, Grace! Get out of there right now! Run as fast as you can. And *hide*. Hide somewhere where nobody can find you. You hear me? I need you to understand."

"I hear you."

"Good," he says. "*Run.*"

The moment he says the word, I hear noises in the hallway outside the apartment door. My vision blurs

106

from panic, the phone hitting the floor. Turning, I rush to the window, shoving it open, the loud groan echoing through the apartment. The voices stall for a second before growing frantic as something slams against door. *Shit.* They're shouting, cursing, trying to knock down the door to reach me inside. I leave everything laying there, knowing I've been caught, knowing there's no time to grab it, not giving a shit about any of it. I climb through the window, out onto the fire escape, and turn to run.

A startled scream escapes my lips, my body trembling, when I damn near collide with someone there. Inhaling sharply with surprise, a familiar scent hits my lungs, and all at once, I know I'm done.

I'm *done.*

My knees are weak and my chest is heavy and there are tears in my eyes I scarcely understand. They blur my vision, distorting the sight in front of me, like my body can't handle seeing who it is. I blink the tears back as I look up, meeting a pair of startling green eyes.

Those eyes.

I know those eyes.

Cody.

The world stops, as I stare at him, seeing his face for the first time in a year. His expression is blank, but those eyes always told stories nobody but me ever bothered to listen to. His face has hardened, aged a century in just twelve months, but I read the softness in his gaze and listen to the confession he doesn't speak.

Behind me, the door shoves open in the apartment, wood splintering, feet stomping along the floor as they coming closer. Each footstep feels like a punch in the chest. Cody just stands there, right in front of me, less than a foot away, blocking my only way to escape. And I'm frozen, because he's here, but I'm afraid, because he's not.

He's standing in front of me, but my Cody... my Cody's gone.

Slowly, ever so slowly, he reaches toward me.

I stand still, so still.

My feet are cemented in spot and my voice won't work.

He grasps the chain around my neck, pulling the locket out from beneath the hoodie. *His* hoodie. His thumb brushes along the snowflake on the outside of it before he pops it open, looking inside.

Nothing.

There's nothing in it.

He stares into the empty locket for a moment before meeting my eyes, snapping it right back closed. He lets go, letting out a deep sigh, as he looks away from me.

Ten seconds.

He gives it ten seconds, before speaking words that make my world implode.

"She's out here," he shouts. "I got her."

Thirty minutes.

That was all I had.

Thirty minutes to say goodbye to my life.

The Marshal stood in front of me in the apartment, while numerous police officers flanked the building, unmarked cars parked all over the street, agents keeping an eye on things to ensure we were safe in here for the time being. He was still talking... he hadn't stopped talking since the moment he introduced himself at the school... but I stopped listening when he said those words.

Thirty minutes.

In class sophomore year, we had this drill during fire safety week—if your house was burning down, what would you grab on your way out the door? They gave us thirty seconds... thirty seconds to decide what was most important to us.

It was an easy decision: I took my memories.

My pictures. My mementos. My journal.

I didn't even need thirty seconds.

But sitting there, thirty minutes ticking away as they waited for me to grab whatever it was I wanted to take, I drew a blank. Because all of that—all of my memories—I wasn't allowed to keep.

I couldn't wrap my head around it.

"It's a mistake," I whispered, blinking rapidly as I shook my head. It *had* to be a mistake. This couldn't be happening. These things... they only happened in movies. They didn't happen in real life. They certainly didn't happen to *me*. "It's all a mistake."

Witness Protection.

Unfathomable.

"I'm afraid it's not," he said, looking at his watch.

109

"Twenty-seven minutes until we're out the door."

His voice was all business, yet there was some casualness about it, like this situation didn't disturb him at all. I clearly wasn't the first person whose life he disrupted, not the first person whose memories he stole. This, to him, was just another day at work.

But this was my life.

"Time's ticking," he said, casually strolling over to the window when I still didn't make a move to pack anything. "Twenty-five minutes to go."

Everything was a blur. I blinked and I was on my feet; another blink and I was running for the door. It was stupid. I knew that. There was nowhere for me to go. I made it as far as the hallway, bursting right out the door, when an officer grabbed a hold of me, shoving me against the closest wall.

BAM

It knocked the breath from my lungs, forcing tears to my eyes as I struggled against the hands restraining me, gasping and shouting. "Let me go! Please! I don't want to go!"

The tears broke free, streaming down my cheeks.

I didn't understand how his could be happening to me.

"Let her go," the Marshal said calmly from the doorway to the apartment. The officer loosened his hold on me right away, slowly backing up.

I glanced over at the Marshal, wiping my eyes, but the traitorous tears wouldn't stop. "I can't… I can't do this. I can't just *leave*. You can't make me!"

He stared at me for a moment, frowning, before saying simply, "You're down to twenty minutes now."

Twenty minutes.

They flew by in another blink. I went into my room and filled up a duffel bag—just one bag was all I was allowed to take. I didn't know what I threw in it, nor did I care. The rule was 'don't pack anything that can be linked to Grace Callaghan.'

The Marshal shifted through my bag when I finished, pulling out a few things and tossing them aside—my iPod, a t-shirt bearing the name of my school, a monogrammed purse that says 'I love New York'. After he was satisfied, he zipped up the bag, handing it off to the officer in the hallway, who disappeared with it downstairs.

Stepping toward me, the Marshal surveyed my clothing before reaching for the locket around my neck. He turned it over, and my stomach dropped. *No.*

"Please," I whispered, knowing he saw the engraving. "Just this one thing."

He said nothing in response to my plea as he flipped it open, looking at what was inside of it. He seemed to contemplate before pulling out the picture, closing his fist around it before securing the locket again, leaving it hanging around my neck. "Time's up."

He let go and motioned toward the front door. I didn't have time to think, barely had time to process anything, when I was ushered out, not having the chance to even look back. I was rushed straight out of the building, toward an awaiting van parked right along the curb. It was black as midnight, and even the windows were all obscured. The Marshal forced me into the backseat and climbed in beside me as engine started up for us to leave.

Glancing out the back window, I stared at the building I lived in my whole life, surveying the fire escape, realizing I'd never see it again... I'd never see any of this again. If these people, if these men, got their way, I'd never step foot in Hell's Kitchen for as long as I lived.

It was what I always wanted, wasn't it?

But no... not like this.

It wasn't supposed to be like this.

I wasn't supposed to be doing it alone.

I was supposed to be with *him*.

Him.

My eyes met his the second that thought passed through my mind, the moment my gaze drifted to the street outside the side window. Cody stood there, just a few feet away from the idling van, where he often hung out with his friends, but today he was alone. Something inside of me lurched, my heart stalling for a beat. Frantic, I tried the handle as I shouted his name, but the door was locked. It wouldn't open and the window wouldn't roll down, so I beat on it, banging my fist against the tinted glass as I screamed for him. "Cody! Cody! Please! Cody!"

He stared at the van like he was staring through it, hands in his pants pockets. His scowl cracked after a moment. Slowly, ever so slowly, his lips curved until he was smiling.

He was *smiling*.

In a blink, he was gone.

The van sped away down the street. I spun

around in my seat, watching out the back window again as the neighborhood faded away and with it, Cody.

"I'd appreciate it if you put on your seatbelt," the Marshal said, ignoring my outburst. "It's my job to make sure you stay safe."

Unlike his son, Cormac Moran hasn't aged a day. He stands in front of me, in the empty apartment, beside the boy I encountered at the library last night. I stand still, trying not to fidget, but my hands won't stop shaking and my heart still hasn't slowed. I stare straight at Cormac, watching him, trying to ignore Cody's presence beside me.

Trying not to fall to pieces because of him.

He slipped in the window behind me after silently motioning for me to go back in where I came from. He's spoken not a word to me. He hasn't even looked at me again. His gaze is trained on the floor, his hands shoved in his pockets, as he waits, like me, for Cormac to do whatever it is he has planned.

I want to scream at him, ask him why he's doing this, why he's being this person I know he's not, but the words are lodged in my throat, beaten back by Holden's warnings that I stupidly ignored. He said I couldn't ever come back here. He said this life was over, that I'd never find here what it was I was looking for. I was a different person this past year. Why would I think Cody wouldn't be, too?

Cormac just stands there, eyes studying me, before his gaze flickers to his son. He stares at him for only a moment, but it's a moment that says so much. He's surprised by his loyalty, surprised that his son didn't just let me go.

I'm surprised, too.

My Cody would have.

"Miss Callaghan," Cormac says, smiling deviously as he turns his attention back to me. "Or should I call you Miss Kennedy?"

I say nothing, trying to fight the swell of sickness that rushes through me at the fact that he knows. He knows that other girl exists, the one I've tried to be, and he somehow knows who she is.

"Maybe we'll just stick with Grace then," he says when I don't humor that with a response. "At any rate, it's nice to see you home again. I love what you guys did with the place."

He motions around us, at the vacant apartment.

I don't find him nearly as funny as he seems to think he is.

"What do you want from me?" I ask, my voice shaking. I don't want to play this game with him. I've already been crushed. I don't need toyed with on top of it.

"I think you know what I want," he says, reaching over and grasping the boy beside him on the shoulder. "To be honest, when I heard from Joey here that you were in town, my first thought was just to kill you. Slit your throat, drop you off a building... you know, send a message to your father. I wanted to... *planned* to... until another idea surfaced."

Hope swells inside of me, mixing with a dash of terror. He might not be planning to kill me right now, but some things are just as bad as death. "What idea?"

"That we could use you for more than just sending a message," he says. "You see, killing you would destroy your father, but maybe if we give him some hope... give him an ultimatum of sorts, tell him we'll let you walk away if he recants... it could work in our favor."

I want to say my father would never do that, but I'm not sure.

"Brilliant, huh?" Cormac grins. "It was my son's idea. Said there was no reason to be hasty putting a bullet through your skull when we could use that pretty face to get something we want first."

My gaze darts to Cody, whose attention is still fixated on the floor.

"So settle in," Cormac continues. "This will be your home again until we're done with you. Joey will take first watch. You know, make sure you don't try to disappear out the window."

Cormac turns, heading out the door, leaving it open behind him. Cody hesitates for a second before starting after his father, pausing only briefly to bend down and pick something up. My phone, I realize. I'd dropped it when I was talking to Holden. Cody snaps it closed, his eyes drifting my way, meeting mine for only a second, before he slips the phone in his pocket and walks out.

I stare at the broken door after it closes. Joey walks over, leaning back against it, securing it with his body since they broke the locks coming in. He crosses his arms over his chest, regarding me.

"Get comfortable," he says. "It's going to be a long day."

A long day it is.

Minutes feel like hours.

Joey tries to talk to me, to pass the time, but I have nothing to say. I slide right back onto the floor, watching the shadows from the sunlight move across the room as the day fades away. It's cold and my stomach hurts. Adrenaline and fear nauseate me, bile burning the back of my throat.

Giving up eventually, I lie back down, huddling into a ball and wishing this all would go away. I close my eyes, squeezing them shut tightly, letting the blackness of sleep take me.

"Gracie."

My name, whispered in that voice, feels like a dream. A long ago memory. Sudden warmth swaddles me. I wrap myself in it, getting lost in the sensation, until I hear it again. That voice. My name.

"Gracie."

My eyes snap open. I'm greeted by darkness, a reality that's ugly and bitter cold. Gasping, I sit straight up, my back pressing against the wall. Confusion rattles me. A thick blanket covers me. Crouching down right in front of me is *him*.

Cody.

It takes a moment for the world to come back into focus, for me to remember how the hell I got to this place. My eyes scan the room suspiciously, looking for Joey or Cormac or somebody else... anybody... but it's only him. They must've traded off watch while I was sleeping.

"I brought you something to eat," Cody says, holding out a bag of take-out. "Figured you must be hungry."

Carefully, I take it from him, setting it down on the floor in front of me. I don't look inside. I'm not going to eat it, whatever it is. Cody seems to realize that and frowns, standing back up and turning away from me.

I'm not sure why I expect him to leave when he reaches the door, but he doesn't, instead sitting down on the floor beside it, back pressed against the wall. He pulls his knees up, resting his arms on them, while I pull the blanket up around me, shielding myself with it, blocking out some of the cold. I'm not sure where it came from, but I'm assuming from the same one who brought me food.

We're alone.

That realization does something to me, twisting my insides in knots. My anger and fear tinges with something else: *betrayal*.

I don't say anything to him.

I don't know what to say to this boy.

After a while, Cody clears his throat. "It was the library, you know."

I look over at him with confusion.

"You used the name at the library—Grace Kennedy. Joseph saw it written on the sign in sheet and put the pieces together. One of your neighbors said they heard noises up here in the apartment, and well... here we are."

I'm kicking myself for not considering what name

I used at the library, but in the grand scheme of things, that feels inconsequential at this point. Cormac already has me. Finding me isn't really a concern anymore.

Silence surrounds us. It's awkward. For the second time in my life, I find myself nervous in Cody's presence. Pulling my legs up, I wrap my arms around them, laying my head on my knees. I face away from him, staring blankly at a wall.

"I've thought about you," he says quietly. "Every day. I still come around here sometimes, just hanging out on the corner across the street. I knew you left, but being here, being where you used to be… it still made me feel close to you."

I don't know if those words are meant to comfort me, but they only make everything about this feel worse. Tears sting my eyes, and I try to fight them, try to contain them, but the hurt just runs too deep.

"I never wanted it to come to this," he continues. "You have to believe me, Gracie."

"Don't call me that," I say, tears streaming down my cheeks. *Gracie.* The word is like my Kryptonite. I don't want a thing to do with it. "Please. Just… don't."

He sighs so loudly it seems to echo through the room. Brushing my tears away, I glance over at him, seeing his face is now covered with his hands. Defeat slumps his shoulders, and I know I shouldn't care… I *shouldn't…* but we've always been so connected that we shared pain.

Old habits are hard to break.

He pulls himself together after a moment, sitting up straighter, his expression going stone cold. Slowly, he reaches beneath his shirt, into the waistband of his pants, pulling out the last thing I ever expect to see in his hand.

A gun.

I'm so woozy I feel like I might pass out.

He holds it in his lap, tinkering with it in the darkness, the click-click-click of the cylinder as he spins it tightening my chest, confirming what I feared. My Cody—the boy who loved to use his fists when words just wouldn't suffice—had never touched a gun in his life.

Hours pass.

Maybe it's minutes.

Days. Weeks. Months. Years.

My life is a ticking clock that's destined to stop eventually.

Eventually Cody gets to his feet, tucking the gun back away as he strolls across the room. My gaze trails his feet, refusing to meet his eyes, even when he pauses right beside me. He shoves the window open, and I shudder at the blast of cold air that sweeps inside. Pulling the blanket tighter around me, I shiver, watching as he climbs out on the fire escape.

He pauses there, right outside, so close I can still see him, so close he could hear me if I tried to run. My eyes drift to the door anyway, scanning it instinctively, wondering how easy it would be to escape. I could make it to the hallway before he even made it back inside.

I know this building better than Cody.

I navigated it nearly my entire life, while he was never allowed inside.

I could run, and he might never catch me.

All I'd need to do is make it outside.

"He's here," Cody says, just loud enough for his voice to filter in the open window, with it the subtle familiar scent of smoke. "Cormac's sitting downstairs in his car, watching, waiting... fuck, I don't know. I don't know what he's doing. But he's here. So you can try to run if you want, but you won't make it very far."

After all the time, he's still in my head.

I almost feel violated, but he just spared me from more pain.

I would've done it.

I would've tried.

Ten more seconds and I would've been out the door only to be caught the second I stepped outside.

"Wonderful," I mutter. "Probably sitting down there planning my execution."

Cody shifts around, one leg draping over the windowsill, dangling inside as he gazes down at me. I don't look at him, but I can feel his eyes trained my way.

"You really think I'd let that happen?" he asks, smoke filtering inside the apartment as it rolls from his lips when he speaks. "You really think I'd let Cormac hurt you? That I'd let him kill you?"

"I don't know," I whisper, and it's true. I don't know. I don't know what kind of person this Cody is. I don't know if he still has a heart.

Cody laughs bitterly under his breath. "You should know. You should know *me*."

"I thought I did."

120

Cody tosses what's left of his joint away, not bothering to put it out, and slips back inside. My breath hitches when he crouches down beside me, so close I can smell him again. Slowly, my head turns his way, and his face is so close my nose nearly brushes his. His eyes burn so bright, so green and alive, even if they're now slightly bloodshot. This close, he still looks like my Cody. This close, I can still see his soul inside.

"I'm the same person, Gracie," he says, matter-of-fact, putting stress on that name even after I told him not to call me it. "I just grew up."

Before I can even process what he said, his hands are cradling my face, palms pressed against my cheeks. I feel my skin grow warm beneath his cold hands. I want to yank away, to put some distance between us, but my muscles are suddenly frozen. My lips part, and all I can do is gasp as he slowly, slowly leans toward me, inching closer to my mouth, so close I can feel his breath.

Inside of me is anarchy.

Butterflies take flight in my stomach, every inch of me tingling from his touch. One of the most terrifying days of my life, and somehow his presence wipes away the fear. He's one of them, and I hear the warnings in my head, but my heart still doesn't understand.

How can I still love him so much?

What's wrong with me?

"You know me," he whispers, the words barely a breath. "You always have."

It's smoke and mirrors, I tell myself, a trick of

121

hand from a sneaky boy who's playing a dangerous game. Words are just words, but somehow, I feel them. I feel them seep through my skin, settling inside of me like they're actually true.

"What are you doing, Cody?" I ask quietly as he inches even closer, his lips so close to brushing against mine.

He stares into my eyes for a moment before whispering, "What I have to do."

I don't have time to question what that means. A shrill ring echoes through the apartment, shattering the moment. I exhale sharply as Cody's hands instantly leave my skin. He stands up, putting that much needed space between us.

Stepping back, he reaches into his pocket, and I tense when he pulls out a phone. My phone. It's ringing. *Holden.* Cody flips it open, and I start stammering, words catching in my throat when he reaches for the button to answer it. *Shit.*

Bringing the phone to his ear, he stands in silence, staring down at me as he does. I can faintly hear a voice streaming through the line, Holden speaking, but Cody doesn't react. He merely listens for a moment, his expression blank, before he clears his throat.

"You want her," he says, "come get her."

That's it.

That's all he says.

He doesn't even give Holden a chance to respond.

Cody snaps the phone back closed and drops it to the floor in front of me. I pick it up, surprised he lets me have it back, but he's already preoccupied. His hand is in his shirt, and I realize he's clutching that gun again. He pulls it out, and my heart races frantically when he holds it tightly in his hand. There's noise in the hallway, voices I realize belong to Cormac and someone else.

Cody startles me then when he grabs my arm and yanks me to my feet. I barely have time to steady myself when he's shoving me toward the open window.

"Go," he hisses. "This time, it's your turn to run."

"But—" I try to dig my heels in, confused, but he's stronger than I remember him being, or maybe I just grew weak. "I don't understand. I thought you said... I mean..."

"There's no time for this. Get the hell out of here while you can."

He pushes me through the open window, but I stall there, refusing to go any further as I turn to him. "Come with me."

"I can't."

"Please. Just... come along. Run away with me. We can leave together. We always said we would."

"Now's not the time for childish dreams, Gracie," he says, a hard edge to his voice. "You need to run."

"But—"

My argument is silenced abruptly when he pulls me down, yanking part of me back through the window, smashing his lips to mine. I freeze as he kisses me deeply, not the soft kisses from him I was always accustomed to. He kisses me like he needs it as much as the air he breathes, like he might die of thirst without a taste of my lips. It's a kiss that says hello and a kiss that says goodbye, a kiss that covers every moment in between… a kiss that brings tears to my eyes.

It's the kind of kiss you give someone when you need it to last a lifetime.

It's over quick, just as the door to the apartment behind him opens. He shoves me hard, making me stumble across the fire escape. "Go!"

I don't want to go.

I don't.

But I know he's giving me a chance to escape, and that's not something I can waste. Turning, I bolt down the steps, only making it a few floors before chaos erupts. Looking down, I watch as cars swarm the neighborhood, vibrant lights filling the afternoon sky like they had done a year ago outside of my school. I'm frozen, my eyes trailing the turmoil, as SWAT teams descend upon the building.

It's only a minute—maybe less, I don't know—before a loud bang rocks the neighborhood, so violent it shakes the fire escape. I grip onto the railing, my stomach sinking, as my gaze darts up toward the fifth floor. Through the open window I hear the shouting, the succession of bangs that sound like gunshots. My heart is in my throat and my knees are weak, nearly giving out on me.

Anarchy lights up the apartment, rivaling what I feel deep down in my soul. I scream at the top of my lungs, scream for Cody. Frantic, I try to run back up the steps, everything falling into a haze, when the fire escape rattles around me, arms encircling my waist.

For a moment, I think they're his.

I think somehow he made it down here.

Somehow he's here.

But the arms aren't right, they're too heavy, and the smell is so different, like too-strong mint. A familiar voice tries to soothe me, the only voice who spoke to me for almost a year.

"Calm down, Gracie," Holden says. "You're okay."

"Cody!" I scream, trying to fight my way out of his grip, but I can't. He hauls me off the fire escape like I'm made of nothing, pushing me into the back of an unmarked van idling along the curb. It happens in a matter of seconds, faster than the first time I was whisked away, but this time there's more fight in me.

Maybe I'm stronger than I thought.

"Stop the car," I scream, tears streaking my cheeks as I lash out, trying to open the doors as the van speeds away from the apartment building. I'm trapped, but I'm not going to surrender... not after what just happened. I ball my hands into fists and strike out at Holden, screaming at him. "We have to go back! We have to go back for Cody!"

Holden blocks my punches, waving off the concerned looks from the driver of the van. I consider unleashing my rage on him, jumping into the front seat and making him turn the goddamn vehicle around, when Holden snatches me by the arms, restraining me. "Calm down."

"I can't!" I scream. "We can't leave Cody there!"

"We have to," he says. "He knew what he was getting himself into."

I don't want to accept that answer, but he doesn't give me much of a choice. He threatens to handcuff me if I swing at him once more.

I fall apart in the back of the van, crying as I shove away from his arms. I don't know what's happening and Holden isn't uttering a word. I don't know if Cody is hurt, if he's alive, if he was going down with his father. I don't know what the hell happened, why he let me go, if he'd meant to all along or if seeing me again brought out the boy I used to know.

I don't know.

I know nothing.

The van speeds out of Hell's Kitchen, following a familiar path, the same one we took last time.

After a moment, Holden starts patting me down, feeling me up, like I'm a perpetrator and he's looking for guns. "Where's your phone, Gracie? Please tell me you have your phone."

Frowning, I reach into my pocket and grab the phone, throwing it at him. It whizzes by his head, smashing into the side window, but of course it doesn't hurt anything. The glass is shatterproof. I know—I've tried to break it. Holden doesn't flinch, picking up the phone when it lands on the floor. He flips it right over, pulling off the back, and lets out a deep breath. "Thank God."

I watch as he pulls something out, something the size of a fingerprint, and holds it up. It's some kind of microchip, one of the smallest I've ever seen.

"What is that?" I ask.

"This, Gracie, is *justice*," he says. "This little card holds all of Cormac Moran's secrets, every dirty deed he's done over the past year."

126

I stare at it, stunned. "How did it get in my phone?"

As soon as I ask that question, I know. I know how it got there. *Cody.*

"He called me," Holden says, "earlier today, from your phone. He said you were okay, that he was keeping an eye out, and he arranged for us to come for you. He said he had information... more information than he had a year ago."

I gape at him. "What?"

"He gave us information last year, Grace... information that helped take down his father's organization... information that gave us *your* father, information strong enough to make him turn. But this, the information on this chip... this is enough to take down *Cormac.* He put his ass on the line, you know, and he sent it out with you, just in case."

"In case of what?"

Holden's attention is fixed to the small microchip. He's quiet, like he doesn't want to answer my question, and I don't need him to. Not really. I know why Cody sent it with me, but I want to hear the truth.

I want him to say it.

I hold my breath as he does.

"In case he doesn't make it out of there himself."

"Snowflake," I said with disbelief, staring at the Marshal as I stood in the dusty front yard of an old house in what looked like the middle of the damn desert. It was scorching hot, and I was sweating, and he had to audacity to tell me I was now a resident of a town called *Snowflake*. "You're kidding."

"Not kidding," he said. "Snowflake, Arizona... population 5,590 at last count, so I guess that makes you 91."

"Snowflake," I said again, looking away from him to glance around. I couldn't see any other houses from where we were standing. Less people lived in this entire town than lived on just my block back in Hell's Kitchen. "Look, Inspector—"

"Holden," he said. "Not Inspector, not Marshal... just Holden."

"Look, Holden," I continued, "I appreciate this and all, but I don't think I can live here. No, I *know* I can't live here."

"It's a nice town," he said. "Quiet, quaint... the people are friendly and mind their own business. The crime rate is low and the weather is nice. It's everything you could ever ask for."

No, it wasn't, I thought.

I would ask for *so* much more.

"Besides, I thought you'd get a kick out of it." Holden smiled playfully as he reached over, tugging on the locket around my neck. "Thought you liked snowflakes."

I took a step back, away from his reach, and grasped ahold of the empty locket when he let go of it. I said nothing. What could I have said?

He would never understand.

Sighing, he took a step toward me, closing the

distance I just put between us. He was persistent; I'd give him that. "I know it's going to be an adjustment. You're only seventeen and your life has completely changed."

Almost seventeen and a half now, I thought, but I didn't correct him.

"But you'll get used to it," he continued. "And who knows? Maybe this is all a blessing in disguise. Life works in mysterious ways, Gracie."

I was taken aback by his usage of that name. "Why'd you just call me that?"

"What? Gracie?"

I flinched when he said it again. "Yes."

"The locket," he said. "It's written on the back, so I assumed you preferred it."

I did prefer it, but I kept that to myself.

Another thing he wouldn't understand.

I preferred it because Cody called me it.

Nobody else ever did.

I never wanted this life.

The pale girl with the bright red hair... I never wanted to be her. Even when she's wearing makeup, when she has a reason to put on dresses and nice shoes, I was never very comfortable in her skin. I never wanted to be the girl who navigated the world alone. I didn't want to have to settle for less than what I believed I deserved. I had a wall of dreams and a give-them-hell attitude, and I had plans... plans I wanted nothing more than to see through.

I never wanted to be in this place.

But I never truly belonged *there*, either.

Home was never Hell's Kitchen. Home was somewhere where I could see the stars, where I could stare up at the sky and know, with just a glance, that there was something else beyond this all. Home was the one place I felt safe, and protected, where even surrounded by brimstone and hellfire, I could feel Heaven's touch on my face.

Home.

I miss it.

I miss so much of it.

I miss the smiles.

I miss the snow.

It's been a little over three weeks since I was dragged back out of the neighborhood I grew up in, kicking and screaming, whisked away to a new life, another new beginning, where I had to learn to be another new girl. They took me straight to the intake center in Washington, processing me back into the system, this time as a bona fide witness.

Grace Kelly.

I chose it because of the Princess of Monaco, hoping I'll live at least half the life the real Grace Kelly lived. She left her world behind for a new adventure, walking away from the thing she wanted most for something else, something I like to think she eventually loved even more.

I hope that'll happen for me.

With my new name comes a new placement, something I knew, but something I don't want to think about. I'm not supposed to know when it'll happen. I'm not allowed to know where I'm headed after this. All I know is that for the moment, I'm back here… back in this place.

Snowflake.

I stand along the side of Highway 77, a few yards south of the city limits sign, leaning back against the side of Holden's black Dodge Charger. It's near nightfall, the sun having gone away. In fact, it hid most of the day.

It's amazing how quick things can change. I was gone for only a few days, but when I returned to Arizona, nothing was the same. Winter had moved in practically overnight, ushering in the second I ran out. Gone was the scorching sun, replaced with a ground covered in frost and a cloud-covered sky.

It feels colder here than it felt in Hell's Kitchen. The nippiness in the air makes my nose run and my skin tingle with pins and needles. I'm wearing the hoodie, my hands pulled up inside the sleeves, the hood over my head, pulled down low, shielding my eyes, mostly because it's cold, but partly because I still don't want anybody to look at me.

It smells like him again.

Or maybe my mind is playing tricks on me.

My gaze is off in the distance, far down the highway as it disappears into the growing darkness. I'm so emotionally worn down that I'd give about anything to be anywhere but here right now. It's Christmas Eve, and I'm standing along the side of the road, while nearly everyone else in the world was at home with the people they loved.

"We can wait in the car, you know... if you're cold."

My head turns, eyes seeking out Holden when he speaks. He's standing in the middle of the road, near the broken yellow line. The highway is vacant. We've been out here ten minutes and I haven't seen another car yet.

"I'm fine," I say quietly. "How much longer is it going to be?"

He shrugs a shoulder casually, hands in his pockets, as his pristine dress shoes toe the asphalt, kicking small rocks off of the highway. "Shouldn't be much longer, I'd say."

He hasn't told me why we're out here, why he drove me to this spot or what we're waiting for, but I think I know. Contrary to how I acted when I ran straight into the arms of danger, I'm not an idiot. I think it's time... time to move on.

Because with a new placement comes a new handler. Holden's job ends right here, at the city limit of Snowflake, where he kept Grace Kennedy safe. Grace Kelly belongs elsewhere, the responsibility of someone else.

That makes me sadder than I thought it would.

Another person I'll leave behind, never to see again.

"Do you have a family, Holden?" I ask curiously. I've never given his life outside of his job much thought. Tomorrow's Christmas... doesn't he have anyone waiting somewhere for him?

"I have a brother," he says. "Other than that, no."

"No wife? No fiancé? No girlfriend? Nothing."

"No."

"Why not?"

He shrugs. "Guess I'm already married to the job."

"But you get laid, right?"

The question comes out of nowhere. I feel like a fool the second it's vocalized, but he laughs, not offended in the least.

"I do just fine," he says, shaking his head, grinning. "But I don't think that's a conversation we should be having."

"Because you're my handler?"

He narrows his eyes. "Because you're practically my kid."

That wasn't the answer I expected, but I'll accept it.

A few minutes pass. I'm shivering, clenching my jaw tightly to stop my teeth from chattering so much. Holden doesn't suggest we get back in the car again, even though it's obvious I'm cold. He doesn't seem bothered by anything, his eyes watching me curiously until subtle lights shine down the highway from the south. We both glance that direction, and I watch as the black van slowly approaches, the headlines illuminating us.

I recognize it.

It belongs to the Marshals.

The windows are as black as the paint.

It creeps to a stop a few yards in front of us. I can faintly make out the man sitting in the driver's seat. My eyes shift from him to Holden, who still stands in the middle of the road. He, too, looks away from the van, glancing at me, and offers a slight smile, but

133

there's sadness to it.

"I, uh…" I'm not sure what to say. I want to say so much. I want to thank him. I want to apologize. I want to tell him I appreciate everything he's done for me, that he's shown me more respect and kindness in one year than my father did my entire life. I want to tell him that even though I didn't like being this girl, even though I didn't like being in this place, I did like him.

I want to tell him I don't want to go.

I don't want to go, because when I do, I'll officially have nobody.

I want to say so much, but I say nothing.

His smile dims a little, the sadness taking over as he nods, whispering, "I know."

Tears sting my eyes as they build, but I fight to keep them from flowing down my cheeks, not wanting to fall apart over this. Not in front of him, anyway. He clears his throat, taking a step toward me, his hands still in his pockets. Down the highway, I can hear a van door slide open.

"I have something for you," Holden says. "Something you might want."

I shake my head. "I don't want anything from this life. None of it matters to me."

The clothes, the air conditioner, the shitty car that's still parked somewhere near the airport—I don't care about any of those things. They all belong to that other girl.

The smile that faded just a moment ago returns. "It's not from *this* life, Gracie. Call it a Christmas present."

Pulling his hand from his pocket, he holds it out toward me. I stare at it, eyes widening when I see the tiny picture lying on his palm. Instinctively, I reach for the locket around my neck, a locket that's been empty since he took that picture from me. My eyes dart between his hand and his face, stunned.

"But you said I couldn't have pictures," I whisper, losing that damn battle with my tears as I take it from him. I gaze at it for a second, my chest trying to cave in at the sight of Cody's face. "You said I couldn't keep it because of him."

"You're right—I did," he says. "But that's not going to be a problem anymore."

Brow furrowing, I stare at him with confusion as he subtly nods toward the van. My head slowly turns that way, something inside of me twisting when I see the person standing in the road beside it. It's getting dark, and his face is obscured by shadows, but I know that body. I know that stance. I'd recognize it before I even recognized myself.

"Cody?"

His name bursts from my chest, cracking when it escapes my lips, echoing out in the form of a question, but it's senseless. I know the answer. I know him. His head lifts, green eyes meeting mine. He's so close, so close I can see the slight pull of his lips, slowly morphing into a smile as he mouths my name. "Gracie."

I don't think.

There's nothing to think about.

There's no hesitation.

I don't need ten seconds.

135

I launch myself at him, running as fast as I can, closing the distance between us in a blink. He braces himself when I slam right into him, wrapping his arms around me, pulling me into his embrace. My tears fall like rain as I cling to him tightly, fisting the back of his jacket, burying my face in his chest.

"Gracie, Gracie, Gracie," he chants, one hand resting on my back while the other settles on my head, holding me against him, whispering just my name.

We stand there for a lifetime.

Forever passes in just a blink.

I'm shivering, and shaking, crying, and clinging, and it's Cody who keeps me warm. It's Cody who keeps me on my feet, Cody who keeps me from falling when my knees get weak. It's always him, and I hate myself for doubting it for even a second, but that was that other girl, I tell myself... the other girl who didn't know herself, much less know him. But right here, right now, it's just us. Just Cody and I, the way it was always meant to be.

I feel like I'm home, even though I have nothing that belongs to me, because Cody gives me roots and makes me want to grow and grow and grow again.

"I'll be damned, Gracie," he says quietly. "We made it snow."

I pull away from him, glancing up, unexpected laughter escaping through my tears when I see the snowflakes. It's actually snowing in Snowflake. Spinning around, I start to call out for Holden, amused he'd been telling the truth, but the highway is empty.

The Charger is gone, with it Holden.

I hadn't heard him leave.

Hadn't seen his headlights.

He said not a word to me.

I didn't get to say goodbye.

I stare at the spot where the car had been parked before my eyes drift toward the city limits sign. The man climbs from the front of the van, clearing his throat as he introduces himself. Inspector something, I don't know. I don't care. I look away from Snowflake, at the van, a van I know I'll be leaving in.

I don't put up a fight.

It doesn't matter where I'm going.

Not as long as where I'm going, I have *him*.

Maybe, I think, wishing isn't for fools.

Because sometimes, when you least expect it, they find a way to come true.

9911959R00078

Printed in Great Britain
by Amazon.co.uk, Ltd.,
Marston Gate.